## The Precious One Is Coming Back

---

SHERALEE SNOW

Copyright ©2015 Sheralee Snow
www.thewebelieveseries.com
Self Published

All rights reserved. No part of this publication may be reproduced, stored in a retrieval system, or transmitted in any form or by any means, electronic, mechanical, photocopying, scanning, or otherwise, without the written permission of the author.

ISBN: 978-0-9912175-4-0 (paperback)
ISBN: 978-0-9912175-5-7 (hardcover)

Printed in the United States of America

Logo design by Brandon-Rashad Kenny
Cover design by Nicholas "Nick" Bartley

## *We Believe*
### *The Precious One Is Coming Back*

- *Well written*
- *Biblically sound*
- *Faith based*

—Rev. Dr. Patricia P. Pace
Redan United Methodist Church
Lithonia, GA

*Your words were profound and have inspired me to hope for better in myself through God Almighty through Jesus Christ, who is coming back. I want to run a good race to the finish line.*

—Mr. Jerome Waters
Sacramento, CA

# Introduction
## *Why I wrote this book*

GOOD and EVIL have always been the problem with the human race. God had to save his chosen people from the evils of the world because sin was growing without an end through all generations, and God will not tolerate sin in any form.

Sin started with the disobedience of Adam, the firstborn human created in God's image. Once Adam and Eve had experienced good and evil, the Devil was victorious that day. Sin would be born into all humans and the Devil knew that God cannot accept sin in his Kingdom. God is good!

God already had a plan to deal with evil and sin once and for all, sending his only begotten son, the Precious One, to set the world right. The Precious One's first time on earth was to save sinners and to give us his courses to achieve everlasting life. When he returns for the second time it will be different—his mission will not be to save the sinners. Instead, righteous believers will be blessed and the remainder of the population will remain dead for one thousand years until Judgment Day.

I wanted to expose believers to the truth that when the Precious One comes back, it will be an outcome that many will not be prepared for. God knew he needed the Precious One to save his chosen people that were lost and living in sin. God knew that being born in sin, his people couldn't obey his commandments, but he had a plan for serenity and peaceful living. There was so much evil, sin was spreading like a wildfire, a fire that couldn't be extinguished. In preparing for the End Times, the Precious One left us with prerequisite courses that everyone must pass in order to enter through the gates of heaven before Judgment Day. The believers living in the End Times must pass the prerequisite courses, because we must have the Precious One's Comforter abiding in us.

We live in a critical time when faith must be strong to deal with all the issues we face. Now is the time for believers to do the work that the Precious One left us with. If we aren't striving by teaching, preaching, baptizing, ministering, and showing the love that the Precious One had, we need to start doing a better job. In writing this book, I am using my life experiences to show why I had to get right with God. It's my real life history and stories, and all believers must tell their stories to others. We all have trials and tribulations that have made us closer to God, but keeping them to ourselves is a disservice to God, the Precious One and to others. The Precious One will be back and it will be too late for repentance. Our life history will already have been written, and it can't be changed.

As you read through the chapters, keep in mind the title, *We Believe*. I never discount anyone's faith, as most people *do* believe, but I want you to understand there are many *decisions* you must make to receive eternal life. The choices aren't always easy or apparent, but when the Precious One returns, your life

## Introduction

history should not be a surprise as to your destiny—eternal life or hell.

God left us a blueprint plan to the Precious One's return, and the Precious One left us with an assignment that must be passed to receive everlasting life. The prerequisite courses must be passed with a score of 100%—nothing less will do. Those living during the End Times have time to complete the prerequisite courses, but there will be many obstacles preventing us from passing them. God has given us time to pass the prerequisite courses before the Precious One comes back, as we will read in Chapter 4, concerning God's blueprint plan during the sounding of the sixth trumpet. It is a choice one must make during the End Times, and I hope this book will help us to make the right choice.

I have used the King James Version of the Bible in quoting scriptures. I also address the Almighty Father as God, trying to keep titles simple and consistent. Though God has other names like Jehovah, Yahweh, Allah, the Eternal One, the Father, and many more, I have used the word God. The Precious One is the sacrificial lamb for our sins. The Precious One has been called Jesus Christ, Lord, Savior, Prince of Peace, Emmanuel, and many other names, but I prefer the name the Precious One.

## *Special Thank You*

If I can write a very small bit of Revelation in a book and make it very clear as to God's intentions for ALL people, then I must try to accomplish this difficult but challenging task. I give special thanks in appreciation for all the people who have been instrumental in my life in helping me to finish this book, those living and those who have passed on to a better place. Without your love and contributions to my growth, this book could not have been written. A special thank you to Maxine Blocker (home-going celebration January 2015) and my Great Aunt Emily Collins, whose understanding and Christian faith helped to complete *We Believe: The Precious One Is Coming Back*. A special thank you to Evelyn Dolphin and Marilyn Burkley, without whose skills this book wouldn't have been published in time for *We Believe* to be trademarked. Special love and appreciation to God and my guardian angels—may you all continue to watch and guard over me. I am a servant for God, doing what has been commissioned.

# TABLE OF CONTENTS

Chapter 1: DEVIL'S HEAVEN .................................................. 1

Chapter 2: BLOODLINES ..................................................... 35

Chapter 3: JUDGMENT DAY ................................................. 59

Chapter 4: SOUNDING TRUMPETS ......................................... 87

Chapter 5: MARK OF THE BEAST ........................................ 115

Chapter 6: END TIME WITNESSES ....................................... 137

Chapter 7: WE BELIEVE .................................................... 159

Rebecca,
I hope my book will inspire you as it did to my cousin, Pat Simmons.
*The Precious One is Coming Back!*
Love Sheralee

"God Bless"
A Love Gift from Patricia Simmons
Lancaster, CA.

Chapter 1

# DEVIL'S HEAVEN
## *Good and Evil: can't coexist*

Devil's Heaven—an ugly wretched hole where sin runs rampant. This hole doesn't take away our beliefs, it just puts them on the back burner as we continue sinning. Think of Devil's Heaven as a hole that we create. The Devil smiles because he has captured another soul from God. Devil's Heaven is gathering too many souls! The hole continues to get wider and deeper from troubled souls who are being disobedient to God. Looking around at all the sin that is escalating daily, I wonder why people still continue to disobey God. They continue to rebel against God's rules and commandments, but think they are still going to receive eternal life! I sincerely believe that when people are following their own plan and not God's, they will never find peace, joy, or contentment. I feel that when we disobey God and take matters into our own hands, we enter the hole of Devil's Heaven.

Most people have experienced Devil's Heaven. Who among us hasn't sinned? Even if our loved ones or friends are in Devil's Heaven, we still think that they are good people and will come to their senses soon. Unfortunately, that devilish side emerges, and most people will like it where they are. The question is: Will we repent to get out of Devil's Heaven or will we stay in the hole, continuing to sin? Sinning without repentance carries a high price to pay, but because sin is justified by many, the price tag gets overlooked. If we choose to stay in Devil's Heaven and don't want to repent of our sins, remember this:

> *Now the works of the flesh are manifest, which are these; Adultery, fornication, uncleanness, lasciviousness, idolatry, witchcraft, hatred, variance, emulations, wrath, strife, seditions, heresies, envyings, murders, drunkenness, revellings, and such like: of the which I tell you before, as I have also told you in time past, that they which do such things shall not inherit the kingdom of God.* (Galatians 5:19-21)

If people would just sit back and analyze why their lives are not going in the right direction, then maybe they would realize they are in Devil's Heaven, an ugly hole. We need to repent from our sins to receive God's blessings. We must repent and accept the Precious One as our personal Lord and Savior. Everyone must go through the Precious One to get to God. God hates sin and his Son paid the price for us to have eternal life. It is amazing how and why people continue to hurt each other. Either by words or actions, the hurt is always apparent. People need to sit back and analyze why their hole, Devil's Heaven, is slowly blocking their blessings. I remember telling my number one cousin that the easiest thing to say is "yes" even though you know that the right answer should have been "no." We have become

## Chapter 1 – DEVIL'S HEAVEN

a society of people who want and need to be accepted and not rejected. If fitting in means hurting or destroying one another, then we know why our hole in Devil's Heaven is growing wider and deeper. We need to stand up and be accountable for our decisions and actions. Please learn how to say no. No means we are taking a proactive stance against what people see as normal. How many times have we wished that we would have said NO to the following?

- Selling and/or taking drugs
- Handicapped and racial jokes
- Witchcraft
- Watching your child being abused
- Physical abuse
- Joining gangs or terrorist groups
- Psychics
- Profanity
- Murder
- Stealing
- Lust and adultery
- Lying

We must stop making excuses and begin to be like the Precious One, loving one another. I wrote the following poem, "Plain Simple," because many people mistreat others for no apparent reason. I dedicated it to my mother, who passed away in 2002.

## Plain Simple

If the world could be simple
Like you and me
We'd erase racism
Then we would see

Drop our guard for just a day
Treat people in a Christian way
What a difference our souls would be
Never judging others by the colors we see

A shade of gray
Has fogged the day
As people continue to judge
Through the misty haze

Life has never been
Black nor White
But shades of colors
Glowing in the light

Drop our guard for just a day
Treat people in a Christian way
What a difference our souls would be
Never judging others by the colors we see

Stop staring at differences
Let your mind be clear
Then our souls will shine bright
And colors will disappear

## Chapter 1 – DEVIL'S HEAVEN

> Such an uplifting feeling
> As the fog fades away
> Leaving a clearer vision
> That God is here, today
>
> Drop our guard for just a day
> Treat people in a Christian way
> What a difference our souls would be
> Never judging others by the colors we see

Each of us is accountable when we are aware that someone is hurting another human being. It is time to take a proactive stand against what is considered to be normal. It is easy to take a passive point of view, but hard not to be part of the norm, because it may mean we won't be accepted. It is amazing how we see the beauty in places, but not in people. Things which are addictive to us become an unfulfilled need with no end in sight. The only way to bring an addiction to an end is by becoming a true believer. We constantly judge each other, whether it is over color, religion, looks, health, dress, etc. Why is it so hard to accept each other for who we are? None of us are perfect, nor will we ever be. God said, "Love thy neighbor," not only Black neighbors or only White neighbors. We must erase racism. We must get past our prejudices to understand what God has planned for us. We must become a society of believers who are color blind to the prejudices that we have had. Life will become harder, just as promised in the Bible, and especially during the End Times. We can't change what is to come, but we can try to understand God's plan for a better future. Now let's sit back and analyze why the hole of Devil's Heaven is getting bigger and deeper, and why more souls are entering it.

## DISOBEDIENCE

Disobedience to God has been around for centuries. Since Adam and Eve, humans have been disobeying God's rules, statutes, and commandments. God doesn't accept disobedience. God gave one command to Adam. God told him not to eat the fruit from the tree of the knowledge of good and evil: *"for in the day that thou eatest thereof thou shalt surely die"* (Genesis 2:17). A simple command and not complicated to understand, but Adam ate from the tree. Adam was king of the Garden of Eden. Living in paradise with no stress, no diseases, no headaches, no death, no bills, and no unemployment, Adam and Eve had it made. What man today would not like to trade positions with Adam? One female helper, no competition and no jealousy, and a one-on-one relationship! Adam had favor with God. Adam could walk with God and talk to God, but that wasn't enough for him.

Through Eve, Adam tasted the forbidden fruit. Always wanting something that we know is forbidden, the forbidden fruit of adultery, stealing, lying, or polygamy, is wrong. God created one man, Adam, and one woman, Eve. He did not create two females for Adam or two males for Eve. Disobeying God's commandments, statutes, and rules comes with a high price—our lives. Man has free will, doing what he wants to do. Even the prophets had free will, but they understood the price that would come from being disobedient. Adam forgot all when it came to his one weakness, Eve. Woman has always been one of man's weaknesses. Adam didn't even analyze the pros and cons of his decision. He didn't even have a discussion with his mentor

## Chapter 1 – DEVIL'S HEAVEN

and creator to find out why Eve ate the forbidden fruit. Adam didn't think about the consequences of his actions, he just ate the fruit with Eve. Did he think that the creator lied to him about the consequences of eating the fruit from the tree of knowledge of good and evil? Adam didn't even ask Eve why she ate the fruit.

Eve had it made in paradise, but her life with Adam was not enough. Eve wanted what the serpent told her. She kept listening to that evil serpent in the Garden of Eden. She wanted to be as a god, knowing good and evil. I am sure she thought she wouldn't die from eating the fruit from the forbidden tree. The fruit was probably so juicy and tasty that she just enjoyed eating it without even discussing her decision with her mate.

We do that today, make decisions without discussing them with others. Some of the decisions that others make can cost us our lives. When we make a decision we like to get others to co-sign with us. Eve got Adam to eat, too. When we are doing wrong we try to get more people on our side, the more the merrier. Eve made a decision to take the serpent's word over God's command. The serpent filled her head with lies. When God found out that Adam and Eve ate from the tree of knowledge of good and evil, they began putting the blame on others. Just tell the truth—God already knows it! Adam put the blame on his helper Eve, and she put the blame on the serpent. The serpent didn't care—he'd already gotten Adam and Eve to eat from the forbidden tree. The serpent had accomplished his goal, even though his crime meant he would have to crawl on his belly in the dust!

The devil was victorious and the world would never be the same. The devil won in the Garden of Eden. God must have been so disappointed with his creation! Adam and Eve, who had disobeyed God's command, were about to receive their judgment. Eve would be in pain when giving birth to children, and both she and Adam would die, returning to the ground. Ashes to ashes, dust to dust—that was to be their fate. They had moved outside the will of God by disobeying the one command they were to follow. Adam didn't even realize how much his disobedience hurt the creator. Adam had been created in God's image: *"in the image of God created he him; male and female created he them"* (Genesis 1:27). Adam's disobedience cost the world a lot. Adam was driven out of the Garden of Eden to till the ground to which he would return.

It seems that most people today march to their own desires, forgetting the price that the Precious One paid for us. Death is promised to all, but sin without repentance has a higher price to be paid—no eternal life. God's word is clear and simple. Living outside of the will of God is destructive and the cost is too high. If we want our souls to have everlasting life, we must repent and pass the Precious One's prerequisite courses before the End Times. Disobedience has no place in the Kingdom of God. We need to be obedient students as we study the Precious One's prerequisite courses. We must go through the Precious One to get to God. He paved the way for us to achieve everlasting life and to get to know the God who created all. If we choose to stay in Devil's Heaven and don't want to repent from our sins, remember this:

> *Fools because of their transgression, and because of their iniquities, are afflicted. Their soul abhorreth all manner of meat; and they draw near unto the gates of death.* (Psalm 107:17-18)

Chapter 1 – DEVIL'S HEAVEN

## GOD'S RULES

We must abide by God's book. We can't change his commandments and statutes into our own rules. Just take a look at how we are trying to change God's rules, forgetting that it's God's law which was to be taught and learned. Exodus 24:12 states, *"And the Lord said unto Moses, Come up to me into the mount, and be there: and I will give thee tables of stone, and a law, and commandments which I have written; that thou mayest teach them."* First of all, we need to understand what God said to Moses. The law and commandments written on stone gave a clear stamp that his laws are permanent and eternal for us to learn and abide by. Moses received the laws from God. The Ten Commandments are the natural laws which our heavenly God authored and gave to us. We haven't abided by them and I think we need a refresher course in the "Top Ten" things we should be doing. The Ten Commandments are in Exodus 20:3-17.

> 1. *Thou shalt have no other gods before me. (Ex. 20:3)*
>
> We should be worshipping and praying to one God and him alone. God is a jealous God; God's glory can't be shared with anyone.
>
> *For there are three that bear record in heaven, the Father, the Word, and the Holy Ghost: and these three are one. (I John 5:7)*
>
> 2. *Thou shalt not make unto thee any graven image, or any likeness of anything that is in heaven above, or that is in the earth beneath, or that is in the water under the earth: Thou shalt not bow down thyself to them, nor serve them: for I the Lord thy God am a jealous God, visiting the*

*iniquity of the fathers upon the children unto the third and fourth generation of them that hate me; And shewing mercy unto thousands of them that love me, and keep my commandments.* (Ex. 20:4-6)

Are we making God jealous?

3. *Thou shalt not take the name of the Lord thy God in vain; for the Lord will not hold him guiltless that taketh his name in vain.* (Ex. 20:7)

Do we swear falsely or curse anything in his name? Our God is a God of love, whom we need to love, honor and respect unconditionally.

4. *Remember the sabbath day, to keep it holy. Six days shalt thou labour, and do all thy work: But the seventh day is the sabbath of the Lord thy God: in it thou shalt not do any work, thou, nor thy son, nor thy daughter, thy manservant, nor thy maidservant, nor thy cattle, nor thy stranger that is within thy gates: For in six days the Lord made heaven and earth, the sea and all that in them is, and rested the seventh day: wherefore the Lord blessed the sabbath day, and hallowed it.* (Ex. 20:8-11)

This one day out of seven is God's day. Do we dedicate one day to God, to whom we owe our being, and from whom all blessings flow? Saturday—God blessed this one day out of the week.

5. *Honour thy father and thy mother: that thy days may be long upon the land which the Lord thy God giveth thee.* (Ex. 20:12)

I preached this message at my mother's funeral. I had been blessed to love and honor my mother for 47 years. Understand what this commandment is saying: Honor

## Chapter 1 – DEVIL'S HEAVEN

your mother and father so that your life may be long upon the earth.

6. *Thou shalt not kill.* (Ex. 20:13)

God is the Master, holding in his own hands the power of life and death. Killing is a deadly sin.

7. *Thou shalt not commit adultery.* (Ex. 20:14)

The institution and contract of marriage are very precious in his sight. Adultery is so common today. This commandment has been skipped, overlooked, or forgotten.

8. *Thou shalt not steal.* (Ex. 20:15)

Stole something from someone lately?

9. *Thou shalt not bear false witness against thy neighbour.* (Ex. 20:16)

We should always speak the truth in all that we do in connection with our fellow men. Let our words adhere to complete honesty. Don't slander, defame, or misrepresent another person. Our untamed tongue can be wicked.

10. *Thou shalt not covet thy neighbour's house, thou shalt not covet thy neighbour's wife, nor his manservant, nor his maidservant, nor his ox, nor his ass, nor anything that is thy neighbour's.* (Ex. 20:17)

We can't be this greedy. Taking anything from your neighbor is a sin. Think of a neighbor as a friend and that taking anything from a friend is wrong. What has happened to "love thy neighbor"?

God has given us in one single word the virtue needed to carry out every one of the commandments. THAT WORD IS LOVE. We have forgotten God's commandments and have even changed his rules:

1962: Prayer is banned in school. (www.free2pray.info)

1963: The Bible is banned from being read in schools. (www.free2pray.info)

1980: The Ten Commandments are removed from schools, courthouses, and other public places. (www.foxnews.com)

We have changed so many things, yet we haven't changed something written on our currency: "In God We Trust." I don't think we trust God, do you? How can we have this saying on our currency and continue not doing the will of God? We ban prayer, Bibles, and the Ten Commandments in schools, but were those the right things to do? If students saw and read the Ten Commandments every day in schools, I think it would make a great difference in their judgment. In addition to schools, parents should talk about the Ten Commandments with their children, too. We have lost what God has given us to learn. We have forgotten why we were created and who our mentor is. Now, down through the generations we have Devil's Heaven acquiring too many souls through sin. Souls have lost their savor of salt that made them unique. Matthew 5:13 states, *"Ye are the salt of the earth: but if the salt has lost his savour, wherewith shall it be salted? it is thenceforth good for nothing, but to be cast out, and to be trodden under foot by men."*

Getting out of Devil's Heaven begins by living by God's statutes and commandments. We must walk after God, fear him, keep his commandments, and obey the Holy Spirit. I want all believers to walk through the pearly gates of eternal life. We must all become 100% believers. The Precious One will return and judge us one by one. Understand that the Precious One's role the first time on earth was to preach, teach, and get sinners to repent. He didn't come the first time for the righteous believers, he came for the sinners. Now, when the Precious One returns for the second time, it will be different. We will have either passed or failed his prerequisite courses, as there will be no time to repent when the Precious One returns. The Precious One is going to put an end to evil and establish God's Kingdom and reward the righteous believers.

## BELIEVERS

Looking around at all the sin that is escalating daily, people continue to rebel against God's rules and yet they still think they are blessed and will receive eternal life. In Devil's Heaven the hole is getting deeper and wider because people haven't resisted the devil and they don't want to repent from their sins. There are two types of believers, 100% or 50%. I give all believers 50% and then I give 50% more to the believers that have made it out of Devil's Heaven. Both types believe and know that there is one God and we must repent through the Precious One to get to God. Unfortunately there are differences between a 100% and a 50% believer:

| 100% Believer: | 50% Believer: |
| --- | --- |
| Believes in one God | Believes in one God, hopefully |
| Has sinned but repented and accepts the Precious One as Lord and Savior | Has sinned without repentance, may or may not accept the Precious One as Lord and Savior |

| 100% Believer: | 50% Believer: |
|---|---|
| Is grateful and is obedient unto righteousness | May be grateful, but is very disobedient to righteousness |
| Has dedicated their life to the Precious One and knows who is in charge—is reborn | Is dedicated to themselves—is not reborn |
| Has peace, a true relationship with the Precious One | Has no peace and no relationship with the Precious One |
| Listens to the Holy Spirit | Blocks out and ignores the Holy Spirit |
| Has passed all courses 100% (Faith and Works) | Has failed courses (may have Faith, but no Works) |
| Walks in the light, spiritual identity | Walks in darkness, carnal identity |
| Disciplined and has a servant disposition (serving God) | Has no discipline and is not serving God, mainly serving himself/herself |
| Has suffered through trials and tribulations, but blessed by God | Has suffered through trials and tribulations but is offended at God for trials and tribulations |
| Has received the Precious One's Comforter | Has not received the Precious One's Comforter |

The 100% believers have sinned, but have repented from their sins and accepted the Precious One as their personal Lord and Savior. If they sin again, they repent again—it's a learning experience. The 100% believers have dedicated their lives to God and surrendered their lives through the Precious One. The 100% believers have dealt with Devil's Heaven and they have gotten out of the hole. The 100% believers understand who is in control of their lives, and they have been blessed to receive the Precious One's Comforter, as they passed his prerequisite courses. They have that special glow, a light that can't be blown out. Remember when the Precious One said, *"Drink ye all of it; for this is my blood of the new testament, which is shed for many for the remission of sins"* (Matthew 26:27-28).

The Precious One didn't say for "all," he said for "many."

## Chapter 1 – DEVIL'S HEAVEN

The Precious One knew there would be some 50% believers left behind, as they did not want to repent or get out of Devil's Heaven. Without true repentance one is led to death. The 50% believers may repent from their sins, but their lifestyle shows them still sinning and enjoying the sin. God does not forgive them just because they confess their sins and accept the Precious One as their personal Lord and Savior, while still continuing to sin. God knows their mind, body, heart and soul—we cannot fool God. The Precious One during the End Times will not pass us if we fail his prerequisite courses. The 50% believers are being deceived by the Devil and by their big egos, thinking they will receive eternal life. Remember, Eve was deceived by the serpent (Satan), and 50% believers are in the same situation. The Precious One was the lamb sacrificed so our sins could be forgiven and we would have a chance for eternal life. By continuing in sin, the choice regarding eternal life has already been made by the End Times. Good and evil can't coexist in heaven—a choice must be made. God is looking for his children to pass the Precious One's prerequisite courses by the End Times!

The 100% believers listen to the Holy Spirit, who was given to us at birth. Many don't even listen to the Holy Spirit, though the Holy Spirit will never mislead us. Think of the Holy Spirit as God trying to talk to us. Many people don't even accept the Holy Spirit as a gift from God. Believe this: The Holy Spirit will never guide us wrong if we listen. Many people know that the Holy Spirit has protected them from wrong situations, actions, and even death.

I remember living in Daly City, California in an apartment complex. One day I came home in the afternoon and was doing my paperwork when there came a knock on the door. The Holy

Spirit told me not to answer the door. I made a phone call to my neighbor across the hall, but he wasn't home. I didn't open my door as I listened to that inner voice telling me not to open it. I lived in a security apartment building—if anyone was coming by to visit they had to announce themselves and I would buzz them in.

Later, I had a good friend stay with me until she found a place to live. While I was away, she was at home and someone again knocked on the door. She opened the door and the man was shocked, because my friend was Japanese. This wasn't the person he was looking for, and he left. I went to the office to report a stranger knocking on my door without being buzzed in. The office management informed me that there had been a series of rapes in the complex and that the police had been notified. I was outraged because the office management hadn't warned us about some stranger raping tenants. I know that my friend and I had been blessed by God. I listened to the Holy Spirit and avoided a situation that could have cost me my life.

The Holy Spirit was given to us for a reason, and if we are living in sin it is hard to listen to the inner voice. Our ears become deaf to the Holy Spirit as we block out the inner voice by our sins. We don't like to be told to stop doing something when we are enjoying it, whether it be lusting, stealing, lying, or cheating. It is sin, and it comes with a high price to pay.

A friend told me that repenting from sin means:

1. Regretting that you disobeyed God
2. Stopping yourself from doing it again

## Chapter 1 – DEVIL'S HEAVEN

3. Intending not to do it anymore
4. Apologizing if it involved others, and making it right
5. Taking responsibility to make it right
6. Listening to the Holy Spirit

The 50% believer is straddling the fence between good and evil. On one side is the Precious One and on the other side Satan. The 50% believers do believe, but they continue to justify their sin. Unfortunately, the 50% believers have a "but" in their vocabulary. They justify their sins, as in the following examples:

1. I love my husband, but I want an affair with someone else.
2. I love the Precious One, but I want to get high on drugs today.
3. I love my wife, but I enjoy beating her.

"But" is a word that is sometimes used after a positive expression to turn it around to a negative one. I would like to turn that around, starting with a positive expression and following through to a positive thought or action. I want the 50% believers to say, for example, "I love my wife, but what would the Precious One do about this situation?" I want us to think about what the Precious One would do before we commit to doing wrong. That's the start to becoming a 100% believer, a transformation of our mind. Devil's Heaven keeps us from receiving or hearing the voice inside us. If our life isn't going towards the light of God and we continue in the darkness, we know what the outcome will be. Staying in Devil's Heaven is a choice that we make. If we are enjoying Devil's Heaven, we know and understand what our fate will be at the End Times.

## *Devil's Heaven*

Felt safe secure
Deceiving many
Digging into a hole
That's Devil's Heaven

An ugly, wretched place
Ample time to plan
Lies and deception
Values left behind

Staring into your eyes
Darkness only to find
Devil in disguise
Gripping your mind

Sinking like quicksand
A hole you don't want out
Lustful, evil ways
Devil's got your game

Embedded with unfaithfulness
Being unstoppable
Devil's directing, not realizing
You're out of control

Devil's Heaven
Gives no respect
High self-esteem
No Precious One to be seen

## Chapter 1 – DEVIL'S HEAVEN

Devil's Heaven
The place to be
Devil's got control
Tricking your body and soul

Left the Precious One path
Devil smiling
Another lost soul
Not going to heaven

Devil's Heaven
Devil's Heaven
Lost your soul
And you can't let go

Devil's Heaven
Devil's Heaven
Prayers can't help
Devil's in control

    Every sane person knows where they stand in their faith and works. If we are enjoying Devil's Heaven and wishing not to repent, we know the consequences. God will not bless us for continuing in sin and disobeying his rules. Remember Adam and Eve—God didn't change his rules and commands when they were disobedient to the Word. He will not change his rules for the sinner, and if sinners want everlasting life, they will have to change to his rules!

    50% believers have a lot of work ahead to get out of Devil's Heaven, but with the Precious One in their heart there isn't anything sinners can't accomplish. The devil has a strong hold on our souls, preventing us from seeing the beauty in having an intimate relationship with God. We need to understand that the devil hasn't changed his mission at all. He is constantly trying to turn souls away from the truth of God. The devil is winning, just as at the beginning of time, when Adam and Eve disobeyed God and their punishment was death. Do you think God wants us in heaven when we have sided with the Devil? The Precious One is coming back to deal with the devil—whose side do we want to be on? Time is shorter than we think for the return of the Precious One. Wake up before it is too late!

## MY FAITH

The hardest thing for me was submitting my life completely to God. I knew that I loved God and the Precious One, but it was hard for me to get out of Devil's Heaven. I had been in Devil's Heaven for years, but the Holy Spirit was constantly working on me and God never gave up. I had to accept that even with the Precious One in my life, and walking by faith, God still had a lot of work for me to do. It took me thirty years to understand what my purpose was for God. I can't explain how and when God will reveal your mission to you. My revelation took years for me to understand what God had in store for me. I was happy living in the Bay Area with my boyfriend. We both had good jobs and a lot in common. We had acquired real estate and we were active members with our bay area ski club. Unfortunately, when my boyfriend lost his job through a downsizing, my hole, Devil's Heaven, expanded rapidly. When he lost his job, everything in our relationship started deteriorating fast. My boyfriend, too, had entered Devil's Heaven. I prayed for God's help, but it seemed that my hole just kept growing.

## Chapter 1 – DEVIL'S HEAVEN

One evening at a championship coed softball game, my prayers were answered. My boyfriend had invited his new girlfriend to the game. We were still living together and we played on the same team. This game was very special to our team because our second base player had been murdered by her husband, and we knew both of them. As we were dedicating the game to our deceased player, we had to win this championship game for her son. We wanted to present the trophy to him. Knowing how important this game was, how dare my boyfriend invite his new girlfriend! God is good, because we won the game and only then did I see his girlfriend. I can't imagine what I would have done or how I would have played if I would have known about this first, especially since I played second base, the position of our deceased player. It was after the game that I wanted to fight and confront my boyfriend. My two friends stopped me from a dangerous confrontation.

I knew then I had to leave my boyfriend. My blessings were being blocked by my sins—I was in Devil's Heaven. Living with my boyfriend was a sin and I had to correct it. We must be held accountable for our own life, not for what others do to us. God loves the sinner but not the sin. My life changed that day. God does answer our prayers, even though we will go through trials and tribulations and the answer may not be what we expect! God made me see that my blessings weren't coming from above. I had committed sin, living with a man, and that's not accepted by God's standards. I had to change my situation because I needed God's blessings in my life. I had free will to do whatever I wanted, and I had made bad decisions. I kept trying to salvage a cracked relationship that couldn't be filled in. It was just increasing my hole in Devil's Heaven. When a foundation starts with a crack, it can't be fixed. We must start with a solid foundation. When I repented from my sins, I realized I had forgotten God's rules, commandments and statutes. I knew what God expected of me.

> Proverbs 3:1-8 (KJV) *states: "My son, forget not my law; but let thine heart keep my commandments; for length of days, and long life, and peace, shall they add to thee. Let not mercy and truth forsake thee: bind them about thy neck; write them upon the table of thine heart; So shalt thou find favour and good understanding in the sight of God and man. Trust in the Lord with all thine heart; and lean not unto thine own understanding. In all thy ways acknowledge him, and he shall direct thy paths. Be not wise in thine own eyes: fear the Lord, and depart from evil. It shall be health to thy navel, and marrow to thy bones."*

God corrected and guided me to understand the meaning of repenting from my sins. I had to clean up my life and I couldn't blame anyone for the wrong choices that I had made. I loved God and the Precious One, but I also loved living with my boyfriend. I was a 50% believer. After that championship game, I made it a point to change my life. Reality can hurt, but the truth sets you free. I had my wake-up call from God. I had to clean up my life, understanding that I can't judge others no matter how much the pain hurts. In reality, we are blocking our blessings by judging others.

It was during this episode in my life that I had to stand still and develop a closer relationship with the Precious One. I had to repent of my sins and pass his prerequisite courses. My life changed for the better. I remember my grandmother always quoting the Serenity Prayer: "God grant me the Serenity to accept the things I cannot change, the Courage to change the things I can, and the Wisdom to know the difference." It's that simple! We can't change what we don't control. We control ourselves, and we can change our lives with the help of the Precious One. I needed the Precious One's Comforter in my life. I had to stand still and develop a prayer life with God. God prepared me for my mission. God realized I was ready to go down the path that he directed. I surrendered my life to God and was ready to be an obedient servant. I accepted the Precious One as my personal Lord and Savior. I knew there would be many temptations trying to bring me down and trying to break my spirit. I had to ask myself, "How strong am I?" Philippians 4:13 states, *"I can do all things through Christ which strengtheneth me."* I was ready for my journey. I had become a 100% believer, letting God guide my life, and with God watching my back I had nothing to fear!

## MY MISSION

One sunny Sunday morning as I started towards my dining room, I felt an uplifting feeling come over me. This feeling caused me to humble myself and kneel on the floor. During that moment in time God's Holy Spirit told me what I must do. I had to write a book for all believers, stressing that the Precious One is coming back and that evil will be destroyed. It was as if my life's history was highlighted and every single thing connected together. I felt a surge of warmth all over my body. It was like turning on a light bulb and feeling the warmth that the light bulb radiates. My mind was enlightened spiritually and everything was made clear to me. I couldn't stop the intensity of the moment. It was so strong that I knew what God's direction was for me.

The energy that I had was so powerful that I felt as though it lasted for a long time, when in reality it was a very short time. In that short period of time, God had revealed my mission. My mission wasn't new to me—it was just made known to me clearly. I knew that God had directed my career, not only my career, but my whole life. I can look back and see how everything connected to my mission. God had prepared my journey for over thirty years for me to be able to tell this story. My mission became so clear through my involvement with my family, relatives, friends, and business acquaintances. Those relationships had helped me throughout my life in understanding what God wanted me to do. I was always grateful to God and I wanted to be rooted in his Word.

I saw how smoothly the Antichrist could implement his plan and place his mark on people (Mark of the Beast). I had to write this book to enlighten everyone about how good God is and that he loves us unconditionally. The final battle will be between the Antichrist and the Precious One. The Precious One will win and be the judge for eternal life. The Antichrist will be in control before the Precious One can return. God is very clear as to what will happen to those who take the Antichrist's Mark of the Beast. My book must be plain and simple; because God wants his people to understand the End Times—that if we don't pass the Precious One's prerequisite courses it will be too late for eternal life.

That Sunday morning the Holy Spirit was so apparent. As I

## Chapter 1 – DEVIL'S HEAVEN

left for church I felt a surge of energy. In church that morning, God's Spirit was so apparent. I had a challenging and difficult mission to complete. I knew God was leading my every step. It was not going to be an easy mission because of the subject matter. I had to try and make it so plain and simple that people would understand that we must believe that the Precious One is coming back and we must become 100% believers. God is giving us time to pass the prerequisite courses before the Precious One returns. Please don't straddle the fence, for time is so precious and we never know when our number is up. If we are 50% believers and God calls us home, ashes to ashes and dust to dust is our future.

It felt strange to be commissioned by God on a topic that has always been a part of my life. I always believed that the Precious One would return as promised in the Bible. If we believe that the Bible is God's story, then the Beast (Antichrist) and the Precious One will battle. I must make it clear that I was raised with the King James Version of the Bible. I truly believe that if you are aware of only one higher being or spirit and believe that God sent us his special son, the Precious One, through whom we receive eternal life, then it doesn't matter what religion you are—we are all brothers and sisters in Christ. I believe what matters is what is in our hearts and the love we have for each other.

I was raised reading the King James Bible, but it didn't stop me from reading other books to gain knowledge about God. This book wasn't written to debate any religion, as I believe all religions fall short of the true Church of God through the long passage of time and manmade distortions of God's revelation. I know if something is going on in your life that makes you wonder if this is what God intended for his children, then you must read this book. I had been a believer in God all of my life. I had prayed for him to show me my mission. Now that I look back upon my life, my mission makes perfect sense.

As a child, I was always drawn to Revelation and the End Times. I can remember so clearly asking everyone in church, "Who is the Beast?" or, "When is the Mark of the Beast coming?" I have always talked about the Antichrist and the Mark of the Beast when the Spirit moved me. I could talk nonstop about the subject. I remember talking to my Uncle about the Mark of the Beast. He told me that he hoped he'd be dead before the Mark of the Beast came, because he was too old to run. I smiled, because my Uncle was a blessed man and he understood that his honest reply was that he couldn't take the mark.

My Uncle passed away in 1996. He had so much unconditional love for his family, relatives like me, and friends. I was always over at my aunt and uncle's house, and even though they had ten children, I was their eleventh. That kind of love is what we must get back to!

In my fifty-plus years on earth God has put me through a natural learning process that materialized my mission. Even if the Antichrist doesn't appear in my lifetime, I must inform all believers who have a spiritual ear about the reality of the Antichrist's mark and the repercussions of taking it. The Precious One is coming back and will deal with the Antichrist and his sidekick, the False Prophet. It's important for everyone to understand God's plan for those who will be living during the battle between good and evil. If I make you question whether you are a 100% or 50% believer and can get the 50% believers to stop straddling the fence and join the 100% believers, I have done a

## Chapter 1 – DEVIL'S HEAVEN

good deed. Every believer's mission will become apparent when God is ready. I'm not a pastor or a minister, only a servant for the Almighty Father. I truly believe that all God's children have a mission, a mission that we can't escape when the Holy Spirit speaks, a mission on which the inner voice will never guide us wrong, but rather empower us to achieve the goal.

### *Mission*

One job for you to handle
A mission to achieve
Sent from our heavenly Father
Blessed it's only for me

Yet you bounce back & forth
God trying to plant the seed
Until you surrender to the Precious One
Your mission then you will see

It's time to take the positive path
Sent from high above
Realizing what a special gift
That you felt never worthy of

Oh! What a glorious revelation
Serving our God
Now your mission is clear
Your journey you may fear

Stepping out on faith
Holy Spirit on fire
What a new revelation
Only you can succeed

A surge of energy
Igniting my soul
Can't wait to start
Praying as I go

Testimony of faith
My purpose for living
God always knew
What was my mission

No turning back to the past
Must complete my task
A blessing from God
Can't disappoint or fail

Victory is mine
My mission is one of a kind
Oh what an illuminating feeling
Being blessed by the most high

Though I have many faults, I continue to repent from my sins and strive never to commit them again. It has been a learning experience, and I am so grateful that God has given us the Precious One. I must constantly strive to be like him. The devil is working harder to capture souls, and we must be aware of his mission. I am going through many trials and tribulations in just trying to complete this book. The devil has sent me so many things to stop

## Chapter 1 – DEVIL'S HEAVEN

me from finishing the book. I believe and know that through all the things that have happened to me, without a doubt God has and always will protect me from the Devil. I have an intimate relationship with the Precious One and I have no fear of the evil ones. I think back to all the things that have tried to disrupt my life and I know that God prevented them all. I have been through many things, including surviving minor surgeries on my foot, knee and tonsils. But they were small issues compared to the following:

### *2000 Aneurysm*

*I was scheduled to have my sinus cavities shaved on the upcoming Friday, but a doctor reviewing the x-ray noticed something in my sinus cavity on Tuesday, four days before the surgery. Thank God for this doctor, as it proved to be an aneurysm. It was three months before I had the surgery. I had the best surgeon from Emory University perform the operation. I knew God protected me the whole time. If my ENT doctor had performed an operation to shave my sinus cavities, he would have popped the aneurysm and I would have died from a nose bleed. Since the surgery, no blood is flowing in my right carotid artery going to the brain.*

### *2009 Stroke*

*I suffered a stroke at my family reunion at Elk Grove Park in Elk Grove, California while talking to my aunt. My left side went numb and I knew that I had suffered a stroke. I didn't want to alarm my relatives, so I asked my cousin if she would take me to the hospital. On the way she asked me which hospital I wanted to go to, either Kaiser or Mercy Methodist Hospital. I told her Mercy Methodist. Arriving at the emergency room on a Saturday evening after 8 pm, there was no line of patients to be seen. I was the only patient that night at that time. Praise God!*

The stroke has caused me some damage on the right hemisphere of the brain, but God continues to bless me with loving relatives and great friends to be able to finish this book, *We Believe: The Precious One Is Coming Back*.

The revelation of knowing that the Precious One will return to judge all and to end the battle between good and evil should inspire all to become 100% believers. It's the final battle with the Precious One, who will win the victory! The end of this battle will establish God's Kingdom. God will not let the Devil win this time! He won in the beginning with Adam and Eve but he will not win in the end.

The Precious One will conquer and defeat the Antichrist once and for all. Knowing that the Precious One will return should motivate all of us to get our lives in order and get the blessings of righteousness. We must pass the prerequisite courses that the Precious One has left us to complete. When the end comes it will be too late to pass the prerequisite courses and repent. Our judgment will already have been decided.

Chapter 1 – DEVIL'S HEAVEN

## DEVIL'S OVERTIME

The Devil is working overtime capturing souls. The first person entering Devil's Heaven was Cain. Cain killed his brother Abel, and the Devil started capturing more evil souls in Devil's Heaven. They became members of his Superior Devil Shield Club (SDSC). We can't say, "The Devil made me do it!" In Chapter 30 of her book, *Will America Survive?*, author E. G. White comments:

> *Satan assailed Christ with his fiercest and most subtle temptations: but he was repulsed in every conflict. Those battles were fought in our behalf; those victories make it possible for us to conquer, Christ will give strength to all who seek it. No man without his own consent can be overcome by Satan. The tempter has no power to control the will or to force the souls to sin. He may distress, but he cannot contaminate. He can cause agony, but not defilement. The fact that Christ has conquered should inspire His followers with courage to fight manfully the battle against sin and Satan.*

Looking around at all the works the Devil is involved with, it is no wonder he is working overtime. The Devil knows that he has a short time to capture more souls in Devil's Heaven, and he wants them to become members of his club, Superior Devil Shield Club. So he is working hard at the following:

- Marriages: Divorce is spreading like a wildfire. There is no end in sight to lust and adultery
- Children: No respect for their parents or elders

- Youth: Issues and problems with high suicide rates; no respect for others
- Religion: Destroying faith in God, the Devil's mission all along
- Love: The greatest commandment, but the Devil keeps replacing it with sin
- Racism: So apparent, no hiding it anymore
- Wars: Never seem to end, one battle after another

It is time to open our eyes and see what the Devil is doing in our lives. We need to reverse the Devil's work and do God's work. We need to honor God's commandments and statutes, for time is running out! The hourglass is slowly draining its sand, similar to what the Devil is doing to our souls as time runs out. Our souls will belong to the Devil and there will be no penetrating our brains with the truth.

The Precious One is the only way to God. The Precious One is sinless, the one who made the sacrifice for our sins so we could have eternal life. Once Adam had eaten from the tree of the knowledge of good and evil, humans were born with knowledge of evil. That's why Devil's Heaven does exist; allowing people to commit sins while enjoying it, with no remorse or will to repent. Get our dark side into the light and don't let evil win! Good and evil cannot coexist. God has a plan for the End Times—the Precious One is coming back and he will judge our final exam, passed or failed.

# Chapter 1 – DEVIL'S HEAVEN

Before I discuss the prerequisite courses (Works) that the Precious One left us with, I want everyone to understand why it's the Precious One who is returning. God has always had a plan by which his chosen people would receive eternal life, and he needed the right person to do his will and become the sacrificial lamb for our sins. Hopefully, the next chapter, "Bloodlines," will explain why the Precious One was the only person worthy to come back.

Chapter 2

# BLOODLINES
*Good and Evil: can't mix the blood*

It's amazing how my life has developed. My life growing up was so simple and less complicated. I grew up in a predominantly Black neighborhood. I had the best childhood, and nobody could tell me that I was poor. A close-knit family is very important to a child. When I talk about my bloodline, I'm including my family, relatives, church, neighborhood, and community. People in my neighborhood were concerned with everyone, not just their own children. If my mother couldn't comb my hair, I would walk across the street and my cousin Ellen would finish the task. I actually enjoyed having my cousin style my hair more than my mother.

When I got in trouble, the adult in charge could spank me. If we needed help with school, our family church provided it. If we needed groceries and didn't have the money, our corner grocery store gave credit. Our neighborhood community cared about everyone. That closeness is what I grew up with, that bond that existed was my bloodline. We supported each other with love and kindness. I have never forgotten that positive feeling I got with having blood relatives and friends.

My bloodline to my relatives and friends began with pricking our fingers and making a promise as our blood mixed, creating a strong bond for life. This relationship with my blood sisters and brothers has lasted a lifetime. The closeness and respect we had for each other has been very real. It was so important for me to be connected; having blood brothers and sisters was completely natural for me. I never realized the importance that the power of blood had to me. I looked at fraternity brothers and sorority sisters, realizing they have the same relationship with their line brothers and sisters that I had with my blood sisters and brothers. That bond and closeness is a combination that changes one's life. We have increased our extended family. That positive feeling of belonging to a group of friends that have the same values and protective instincts is overwhelming. At our family reunion in Sacramento, California, I realized that my cousin had a different meaning for bloodlines. One of my cousins was the family historian at our reunions. She stressed that we came from a strong bloodline, telling the story of our great, great, great, great, grandmother. This is the story about Sarah Grey Wilkinson Johnson Buery, as told by my cousin and her husband:

> *Sarah Grey Wilkinson Johnson Buery Thompson was born a slave in Kentucky on January 2, 1824 (California death certificate of Sarah Grey Thompson). Sarah came to California in 1849 as a slave of two brothers, William and Dr. Artemis Wilkinson. She came with her husband Clayman Wilkinson and her three sons, George, John, and Clark Wilkinson. They settled in the Santa Clara valley*

## Chapter 2 – BLOODLINES

*near the town of San Jose. The African-American historian, Delilah Beasley, in her book,* The Negro Trailblazers of California *(Negro University Press, New York; 1919, p. 102), indicates that Sarah was the first African-American woman in the Santa Clara valley. Sarah's first decade in California would see a tremendous change in her life and would set the course for generations to come. The California Gold Rush was in full swing at the time of Sarah's settlement in San Jose. The Wilkinson brothers still acknowledged Sarah and her family as their property, but she was now living in a free state. Sarah struck a bargain with the Wilkinson brothers that any money earned during the daytime would go to them, while any made independently at night would belong to her. Working nights doing laundry for miners, Sarah saved $3,000, with which she was able to purchase her freedom and that of her family before 1852 (obituary of Sarah Thompson,* The Monterey Herald, *February 12, 1921). Although California entered as a free state in 1850, a confusing mix of fugitive slave laws and court rulings in California made the status of former slaves unclear. Shrewdly, Sarah was able to negotiate her freedom before the onslaught of unfavorable laws enacted in the late 1850s. The Wilkinson brothers honored the payments and provided manumission documents to Sarah and her family.*

*After the family obtained their freedom, Sarah's husband, Clayman, and son, John, died shortly after the California state census of 1852. Between 1852 and 1854 Sarah met Theodore Johnson, a free African-American living in San Jose, who had migrated from New York to pursue his own dreams of gold prospecting. They married and in August*

1854, had a daughter, Kathryn Johnson. By 1860, Sarah had divorced Theodore Johnson, who died in San Jose, California in December, 1868, according to Santa Clara County records.

She married Lewis Buery and moved to the thriving gold mining town of Downieville. It was in Downieville that Sarah converted to Methodism in 1861. This would provide direction for her for the rest of her life. By 1870 Lewis Buery had died, and Sarah married John Thompson. Sarah and John Thompson moved to Grass Valley where they lived until approximately 1890. In the 1870 California federal census, teenager Kathryn Johnson was with her mother and stepfather in Grass Valley. The 1880 California federal census and the 1871 Grass Valley city directory place Sarah and John Thompson's home within a couple of houses of the Grass Valley Methodist Church on Church Street. Sarah's older boys had moved out; Clark Wilkinson was living in Colusa County.

By 1896, Sarah and John Thompson had purchased property in Pacific Grove, California, not far from the ocean cliffs (Pacific Grove, Monterey County tax records, 1890-1925). The property address was 119 14th Street, block 39, lot 17. The move was prompted by Sarah's involvement in the Methodist retreats held in Pacific Grove during the late 1800's. The Thompsons would spend the rest of their lives in their own home in Pacific Grove. They maintained a living by renting out rooms and caring for elderly women in their home. John Thompson died around 1911. Sarah would continue to work in her own home, caring for others until her death on February 8,

## Chapter 2 – BLOODLINES

> *1921 at the age of 97 (Monterey County, California death certificate; obituary of Sarah Thompson, The Monterey Herald, February 12, 1921).*

My grandmother's dad was the son of Kathryn Johnson, the daughter of Sarah Grey Wilkinson Johnson Buery. After that story about our bloodline history on my mother's grandfather's side, I looked at bloodlines a little differently. I now realize that we need to discuss our true bloodlines and their origins, because we are all related from the very beginning of creation to that first human made in God's image, Adam.

## ORIGINS

We all through generations come from one earthly father, Adam, who began the first generation. If we believe what the Bible says in Genesis 2:7, then God formed only one man of the dust of the ground and breathed into his nostrils the breath of life, and he became a living soul. Adam gave names to all cattle and to the fowl of the air and to every beast of the field; but there was not anyone for Adam.

> *And the LORD God said, It is not good that the man should be alone; I will make him an help meet for him. And the LORD God caused a deep sleep to fall upon Adam, and he slept: and he took one of his ribs, and closed up the flesh instead thereof; And the rib, which the LORD God had taken from man, made he a woman, and brought her unto the man. And Adam said, This is now bone of my bones, and flesh*

*of my flesh: she shall be called Woman, because she was taken out of Man. Therefore shall a man leave his father and his mother, and shall cleave unto his wife: and they shall be one flesh.* (Genesis 2:18, 21-24)

God created one man, Adam, and one woman, Eve. Understand that the creator created one male and one female. God didn't create two males or two females. Union was with one male and one female from the beginning of man's creation.

Adam lived in the Garden of Eden. The Bible tells us very clearly the geography of the Garden of Eden. The river went out of Eden to water the garden and it parted into four heads. The four heads were as follows (Genesis 2:11-14):

Pison – Surrounding the whole land of Havilah

Gihon – Surrounding the whole land of Ethiopia

Hiddekel – East of Assyria

Euphrates – Surrounding many lands

The Garden of Eden encompassed a huge geographical tract of land. From the above description the Garden of Eden had boundaries in a lot of places. God planted a beautiful and peaceful garden. If the river went out of Eden to water the garden and the river parted into four heads covering the Land of Havilah, east of Assyria, the Euphrates and the land of Ethiopia, it's no wonder that God's garden was so beautiful and perfect.

Concerning our bloodlines, it takes a male and a female to reproduce. First of all, Adam had to be a man of color, consider-

## Chapter 2 – BLOODLINES

ing that the weather where the Garden of Eden was planted must have been hot and humid. I am sure that Adam and Eve had plenty of melanin to help deal with their environment. As we know from genetics, a dark chromosome can create other colors as well as white, but a white chromosome cannot create colors. In humans, melanin is the primary determinant of skin color.

> Melanin is a pigment that is produced by cells known as melanocytes in the skin of most animals, including humans. This pigment comes in different shades, depending on the genetic make-up of the individual. Melanin comes in two basic forms, and can range from yellowish-red to dark brown. Eumelanin is the most common form of melanin, and is brownish in color. The other form is called pheomelanin which produces reddish-brown color that is often associated with freckles and red hair. (http://www.study.com)

It is possible to have two dark chocolate or milk chocolate or white chocolate humans reproduce and through all the generations get all the different shades of colors that we have now. The one common trait that we all have is chocolate—some have more or less than others.

Understand that no race is superior to another. It is amazing to me why various races believe they are superior to others. Some rulers, dictators, leaders, emperors, and antichrists think it is their right to control, enslave, murder, rape, and conquer others. That was never the will of God. It is the members of the Superior Devil Shield Club that have caused death and destruction to others. The attitudes that club members have, have never gone away.

I am sure that God didn't expect a race war when he created Adam or that people would come to feel that they are superior to others. All of us on this earth are the offspring of Adam and Eve; we are molded from the same clay. The various tribes relocated throughout Africa, Europe, Asia, India, etc., reproducing generations of people of different colors. We must look past colors and see the beauty God has blessed us with. God created Adam in His own image, and Adam's seed through generations of time created nations of tribes of different colors. If we believe the Word of God, then God didn't create other Adams in other places. God created one man, made of dust, in one place, the Garden of Eden. He told Adam and Eve to *"Be fruitful, and multiply, and replenish the earth, and subdue it: and have dominion over the fish of the sea, and over the fowl of the air, and over every living thing that moveth upon the earth"* (Genesis 1:28). God knew this would create people of a variety of colors throughout the earth. We must love one another. God never wanted racism—people have created racism. We are all brothers and sisters and come from the same bloodline.

**Garden of Eden**
**Adam** (Man of Color) **and Eve** (Woman of Color)
(Multiplied)

**Seth** (Son of Adam and Eve)
**Noah** (generations from Seth)

**Flood**
(destroyed every living creature except those on Noah's Ark)
**Noah** (Family multiplied) (Man of Color)

Chapter 2 – BLOODLINES

## Language (ONE)
## God intervenes and creates Languages
## Tribes with their own languages are divided & separated throughout the land

God literally relocated Adam and Eve out of the Garden of Eden—disobedience had a high price. But sin just kept escalating: Cain slew his brother Abel, Lamech slew Cain, and men tempted by lust were taking more than one wife. God saw that the wickedness of man was so great and that his creation was evil. It saddened him that he had even made humans. God was going to destroy all living creatures.

We must be thankful that Noah found grace with God. One man, Noah, saved the bloodline. God commissioned him to build an ark of gopher wood. Noah did as instructed and loaded the ark with his sons, his wife, his sons' wives, and every living thing of flesh, male and female. Understand that Noah had one wife and his sons each had one wife—God didn't originate polygamy or multiple wives, man did. Even after God caused rain for forty days and forty nights, God blessed Noah and his sons and said unto them,

> *Be fruitful, and multiply, and replenish the earth. And the fear of you and the dread of you shall be upon every beast of the earth, and upon every fowl of the air, upon all that moveth upon the earth, and upon all the fishes of the sea; into your hand are they delivered. Every moving thing that liveth shall be meat for you; even as the green herb have I given you all things. But*

*flesh with the life thereof, which is the blood thereof, shall ye not eat. And surely your blood of your lives will I require; at the hand of every beast will I require it, and at the hand of man; at the hand of every man's brother will I require the life of man. Whoso sheddeth man's blood, by man shall his blood be shed: for in the image of God made he man. And you, be ye fruitful, and multiply; bring forth abundantly in the earth, and multiply therein.* (Genesis 9:1-7)

God knew that man would continue to sin. He didn't change his ruling even with Noah's family. Noah's family multiplied. Genesis 10:32 says: *"These are the families of the sons of Noah, after their generations, in their nations: and by these were the nations divided in the earth after the flood."*

Understand our bloodline: Noah was the offspring of Seth, through generations, and Seth was Adam and Eve's son. It's very important to understand this fact. Noah was a man of color. God through Noah's offspring created various races and languages, but not racism. God in Genesis 9:19 states: *"These are the three sons of Noah: and of them was the whole earth overspread."* The generations of Noah multiply and multiply, *"And the whole earth was of one language, and of one speech"* (Genesis 11:1). The different languages came from God. In Genesis 11:7-8, the Lord decided to *"confound their language, that they may not understand one another's speech. So the Lord scattered them abroad from thence upon the face of all the earth: and they left off to build the city."*

## Chapter 2 – BLOODLINES

Noah's grandchildren – The Nations referred to in Genesis 10 (KJV)
Descendants of Shem – Elam, Asshur, Arphaxad, Lud, Aram
Descendants of Ham – Cush, Mizraim, Phut, Canaan
Descendants of Japheth – Gomer, Magog, Madai, Javan, Tubal, Meshech, Tiras

We may come from the same bloodline, but that doesn't mean we have the right blood. God wanted his people to multiply and replenish the land. Tribes migrated with their languages throughout the earth, creating races of people with their own languages. It's very plain and simple—all people created on this earth throughout all generations are the offspring of Adam and Eve. These tribes were God's chosen people. Tribes migrated throughout the world. God saw how sin was still out of control, and he destroyed Sodom and Gomorrah because of their wickedness and sinful life. He could have destroyed the whole earth if he had wanted to, but God is good! God knew he had good, righteous humans and they were worthy to be saved. God was still trying to save his chosen people.

## GENERATIONS FROM ABRAHAM

Through generations descending from Noah's son, Shem, Abram was born. Abram was blessed and found favor with God. God changed his name to Abraham. God established a covenant with Abraham:

> *And I will establish my covenant between me and thee and thy seed after thee in their generations for an everlasting covenant, to be a God unto thee, and to thy seed after thee. And I will give unto thee, and to thy seed after thee, the land wherein thou art a stranger, all the land of Canaan, for an everlasting possession; and I will be their God. And God said unto Abraham, Thou shalt keep my covenant therefore, thou, and thy seed after thee in their generations. This is my covenant, which ye shall keep, between me and you and thy seed after thee; Every man child among you shall be circumcised.* (Genesis 17:7-10)

God blessed Abraham and his seed, Ishmael and Isaac. Abraham's sons had the right bloodline. Ishmael was the firstborn son of Abraham. Although Abraham's wife Sarah became jealous of Ishmael and his mother, Hagar, God intervened and told Abraham to let them go. God blessed Ishmael, made him fruitful, and multiplied him exceedingly. God made him a great nation.

Through the generations from Ishmael descended Muhammad and from Isaac descended the Precious One, both from the bloodline of Abraham. God established a strong and blessed bloodline through Seth, Noah, Abraham, Ishmael, Isaac and Jacob. Their bloodlines were already highly favored and blessed. God also blessed Jacob in a special way as he slept:

> *And he dreamed, and behold a ladder set up on the earth, and the top of it reached to heaven: and behold the angels of God ascending and descending on it.*

## Chapter 2 – BLOODLINES

*And, behold, the LORD stood above it, and said, I am the LORD God of Abraham thy father, and the God of Isaac: the land whereon thou liest, to thee will I give it, and to thy seed; And thy seed shall be as the dust of the earth, and thou shalt spread abroad to the west, and to the east, and to the north, and to the south: and in thee and in thy seed shall all the families of the earth be blessed.* (Genesis 28:12-14)

Jacob woke up and was afraid, but he knew that God was in this place. *"and took the stone that he had put for his pillows, and set it up for a pillar, and poured oil upon the top of it. And he called the name of that place Bethel, but the name of that city was called Luz at the first"* (Genesis 28:18-19). Jacob didn't even know that he would be blessed with twelve sons, that God would change his name to Israel, and that his seed would become the twelve tribes of Israel. His seed would spread throughout the earth—west, east, north and south. Through his seed all the families of the earth would be blessed. God blessed the twelve tribes of Israel and they multiplied throughout the earth, and God also blessed the tribes of Ishmael.

### *Bloodlines*

Abraham's blood started strong
Trials and tribulations
With God's covenant
Nothing could go wrong

## WE BELIEVE® The Precious One Is Coming Back

Generations of believers
God blessed them all
Bloodlines of faith
Believers stood tall

To the bitter end
Bloodline generations continue to grow
Flowing through their veins
It was the right way to go

God is right
Bloodlines so tight
The Precious One to judge
Does your blood fit his type?

Type A, B or O
Not the way to go
The Precious One's blood
Must light up your soul

God blesses us with messengers
Noah, Moses, Abraham, Ishmael, Isaac, Jacob, David
And plenty of others too
Bloodline so strong, yet so true

Blood of the Precious One
Bloodline from above
Shed for you and me
Remission of sins you must see

Need the right blood
Blessing that God gave
Only to the Precious One
Only blood that will save

## Chapter 2 – BLOODLINES

God blessed the twelve tribes of Israel as they spread throughout the earth. Unfortunately, sin and evil were still very rampant among the people. The twelve tribes of Israel knew that God had blessed them, but because evil was born in them, God knew he would have to get rid of evil once and for all. Evil was a trait that was part of their character. There were forty-two generations from Abraham to the birth of the Precious One. God realized that it would take his only begotten son, the Precious One, to set the world straight, someone with the right blood. The right blood of the Precious One must flow through our veins. The Precious One's blood was blessed from God and it was the Precious One's blood which was shed for the remission of sins. Eternal life can't be received without the right blood, and the only way to receive it is through the Precious One. We need to be reborn spiritually, not carnally. While Muhammad was born through a human father and mother, the Precious One was conceived by the Holy Spirit and born from the Virgin Mary. The Precious One was the only one born of the Holy Spirit of God and with a mission that would save this sinful world. The Precious One was the only one to have this unique and blessed birth. The Precious One was granted all power by God and he is the only person to return to Earth.

## THE PRECIOUS ONE

The Precious One came the first time to save, not the righteous, but sinners. The righteous were honoring and obeying God's commandments and statutes. They already had the seal of God upon them. God still saw that evil was inbred among all humans and that the power that evil had was hard to overcome.

But he had a solution to deal with evil—his only begotten son. God knew that:

1. The Precious One could not be born with the DNA from an earthly male.
2. The Precious One had to be born from a virgin, untouched by a human male.
3. The Precious One had to have God's DNA—he needed the right blood.
4. The Precious One was human, but had the will of his father—he made his choice to be sin-free.
5. The Precious One could have the human bloodline from David, but he had to have the right blood from God.
6. The Precious One had to be human in order to experience good and evil.
7. The Precious One had to die and be the first one resurrected into God's Kingdom.

Mixing blood to become blood sisters or brothers wasn't necessary. There was never a need to have other blood brothers or sisters when we have the number one protector with the right blood. When we have the Precious One, there is no other blood needed. The Precious One's blood comes with a guarantee for life!

The problem is that we don't know the full meaning of what can wash away our sins—nothing but the blood of the Precious One. When we receive this special blood each one of us becomes a renewed person. We don't act the same. We treat our brothers and sisters with love and compassion. And guess what? We can even turn the other cheek to our enemies! We know who's in charge of our life and the life that we are trying to achieve. The Precious One shed his blood for a reason, and we can't have the right blood if we continue to sin against God's statutes and commandments, because faith and works must go hand in hand.

Let's talk about what it means to have the right blood flowing in our veins, the blood of the Precious One. His blood was *"shed for many for the remission of sins"* (Matthew 26:28). His blood first of all was not shed for all, but for many. There are some who are lost and will not understand how powerful the Blood is. Sins have spread like a rapid fire with no end in sight. We have gotten to the point where we have justified sin. 50% believers are backsliding, while they need to start moving forward. How deep do we want our hole to go? While continuing in sin we can't even think that we have the right blood. Money can't buy us the right blood, yet we need the blood of the Precious One to receive eternal life. We need that special blood from that special person who was sent to save us.

The Precious One was not only *special*, he was *unique* and *anointed by God*. His birth was special—he was born of a virgin named Mary by the Holy Spirit of God. The Precious One's birth had to be unique and different to wake up the world. He was a human being with the right blood. God had a special mission for his Son. The Precious One had powers that were given to him from God. He made his choice to be sin-free. The Precious One had free will, but he could never be disobedient to God. All the Devil's temptations couldn't drive him away from God. He had his mind on business. He did his mission and God was pleased. The Precious One is the only one able to return and destroy the Devil:

> *Whosoever abideth in him sinneth not: whosoever sinneth hath not seen him, neither known him. Little children, let no man deceive you: he that doeth righteousness is righteous, even as he is righteous. He that committeth sin is of the devil; for the devil sinneth from the beginning. For this purpose the Son of God was manifested, that he might destroy the works of the devil. Whosoever is born of God doth not commit sin; for his seed remaineth in him: and he cannot sin, because he is born of God.* (1 John 3:6-9)

The Precious One was born of God, and God's seed can't commit sin. That is why the Precious One was so special. His character was unblemished. He had only good in his soul. That's why God gave us his Son to be the sacrificial lamb for our sins. Evil can't enter the gates of heaven and the Precious One died and was the first to be resurrected into God's Kingdom, a human being to a spiritual being. He is the only one worthy to come back, because he resides with God and sits at the right hand of God, until it is time for him to return to earth. There is no other person born with God's DNA. The Precious One showed those living during his time on earth that if they followed the commandments and loved one another it would be possible for them to pass through the following and reach God:

1. Death (everyone must die)
2. Resurrection (everyone could be resurrected)
3. Spiritual state of the soul (leaving the carnal soul behind)
4. Presence with God (ultimate victory)

This is why the Precious One is the only one to return. The Resurrection was the solution that God gave us, showing the way to eternal life. His death was for us, the remission of our sins. Remember, sin can't enter heaven—there will be no carnal souls there, only spiritual ones. When the Precious One comes the second time, he will have a different mission. He is not returning for sinners, but for the righteous, and to put an end to evil. He will establish God's Kingdom. All believers know that we need to be like the Precious One and to continue striving to do the following:

1. Love God and love our neighbor.

2. Surrender our lives to the Precious One. Become spiritual-minded and not carnal-minded. I Corinthians 15:45 says, *"And so it is written, The first man Adam was made a living soul; the last Adam was made a quickening spirit."* We need the spiritual soul to enter heaven, just like the Precious One.

3. Preach and spread the Good News. The Precious One was a faithful servant. Romans 6:18 says, *"Being then made free from sin, ye became the servants of righteousness."* Most people want to be the leader and rule over others, but with the right blood flowing through our veins, we want to serve others.

4. Remain steadfast through trials and tribulations. The Precious One suffered a lot. II Corinthians 1:5 promises us, *"For as the sufferings of Christ abound in us, so our consolation also aboundeth by Christ."* Through our trials and tribulations believers have a closer relationship with the Precious One.

5. Continue to pray, as the Precious One did.
In Matthew 6:6-8 we read, *"But thou, when thou prayest,*

enter into thy closet, and when thou hast shut thy door, pray to thy Father which is in secret; and thy Father which seeth in secret shall reward thee openly. But when ye pray, use not vain repetitions, as the heathen do: for they think that they shall be heard for their much speaking. Be not ye therefore like unto them: for your Father knoweth what things ye have need of, before ye ask him."

As I stated before, we all come from the same bloodline through all generations, but we need the right blood to enter the gates of heaven. The right blood only comes from the Precious One. Passing the prerequisite courses during the End Times is the only way for us to receive the right blood.

## *Blood of Jesus*

Blood of Jesus
Shed for you and me
Remission of sins
Can't you see

Blood of Jesus
No mixing needed
Permanent blend
For all to receive it

Blood of Jesus
Not to question
Jesus blood
Is the right direction

## Chapter 2 – BLOODLINES

Blood of Jesus
Available for all
Unfortunately when he calls
Many will fall

Blood of Jesus
Blood sisters and brothers
It doesn't matter
If it's your blood or mine

Blood of Jesus
Is what's needed
Not a chance to miss
Eternal bliss

Blood of Jesus
Can't leave behind
Sisters, brothers
United Christian ties

Blood of Jesus
Crucified for all to see
Drink ye all of it
To receive eternity

Blood of Jesus
Jesus died & arose
Leaving a future
For the blessed to find

Blood of Jesus
A dance for two
My life to Christ
Stepping right into

Blood of Jesus
Not a dream or premonition
To stand before the Son of God
Is my mission

Blood of Jesus
Don't be late to sip
A taste of life for the
Heavenly blessed

## THE BLOOD

With the blood of the Precious One our light will shine bright. To paraphrase Matthew 5:16: *"Let our light so shine before men, that they may see our good works, and glorify our Father which is in heaven."* God is the Alpha and the Omega who has written his story from the beginning to the end. God holds the keys to the gate and knows who will enter. God wants everyone to make the right choice between good and evil. This choice was in the beginning and will be at the end. The circle will be completed at the end of time and the victory will be fought by the Precious One, God's only begotten Son, who has the right blood for salvation. The Precious One was the chosen one from birth. God was pleased with his Son, the only human being that could die for our sins and be resurrected as a spiritual being. He is present with the Father as a spiritual being. The carnal mind was never with the Precious One in heaven.

The flesh is so sinful and we were born in sin, yet we can become spiritual souls like the Precious One. We need to open our hearts and minds to a deeper understanding of God. He gave us his only begotten Son to save many souls. Praising God morning, noon, and night should never be a chore. We should always be thankful to God for giving us the Precious One so that many will have a chance for everlasting life. The Precious One's death had to happen, for every human must die. The miracle was in his resurrection from carnal to spiritual. God showed the world his power by raising his Son. Being an obedient Son, all would know that the Precious One has all power and holds the key to eternal life on Judgment Day. Understand what it means at the End Times to be like the Precious One:

1. We must love God and our neighbors.
2. We must repent of our sins and be baptized and humble.
3. We must have the Precious One as our personal Lord and Savior.
4. We must do the work and pass all the prerequisite courses.

The reward is that through death we are leaving the carnal mind and being resurrected to a spiritual mind. This is what the Precious One's death did for all of us sinners who believe. It shouldn't be a difficult decision to get out of Devil's Heaven and enter into God's Heaven. We are born with both good and evil in us. The evil side can't have the right blood—remember, God will not allow evil into his kingdom. The right blood is a requirement for entering heaven. Tainted blood will not get us a pass on Judgment Day. The righteous blood of the Precious One is what we must receive. The prerequisite courses will tell us how to achieve that. Receiving the right blood is going to take a lot of work for the 50% believer during the End Times. Let's review the prerequisite courses that we must pass before the second coming of the Precious One.

## Chapter 3

# JUDGMENT DAY
## *Good and Evil: passed or failed*

Judgment Day will be different for the people living during the End Times. The Precious One is not coming back to save sinners. His mission is to come back to deal with evil and reward the righteous. The Precious One and his followers will put an end to evil. The Precious One is going to put an end to man's rule and establish God's Kingdom. The Antichrist (the Beast), who is ruling during the End Times, and the False Prophet (along with those who worship his image) will be cast alive into a lake of fire burning with brimstone on Judgment Day. More information will be given in Chapter 5 regarding the Antichrist and the False Prophet. The Precious One will bind them for a thousand years. The souls of the people who were beheaded for the witness of the Precious One and for the Word of God, as well as the people living during the End Times who didn't worship the beast or his image and didn't receive his mark on their foreheads or hands, these righteous souls will live and reign with the Precious One for a thousand years. This is the first resurrection (Revelation 20:6):

"Blessed and holy is he that hath part in the first resurrection: on such the second death hath no power, but they shall be priests of God and of Christ, and shall reign with him a thousand years."

After a thousand years, death and hell will deliver up the dead and every man and woman will be judged according to their works. If our names are not found in the book of life, the lake of fire is our resting place. This is why we had better pass the Precious One's prerequisite courses! We all should be part of the first resurrection. God must be crying from above as he knows so many souls will still be lost during the End Times.

## *God is Crying*

God is crying above
With no hope in sight
On a world of sin
Growing from day to night

Looking down upon the earth
Viewing his creation
Not proud of what he sees
A world of sin and poverty

God is crying high above
 A shameful legacy of sin
That continues to spread
Without an end

No peace on earth
No humanly love
No honoring
God above

## Chapter 3: JUDGMENT DAY

Created in his image
Never measuring up
Continuing to disobey
God's statutes and commandments, any old way

No wonder God is crying
From heaven above
The world has become so
Loveless, evil and gray

Forgotten God's commandments
For us to obey
Statutes, terms and conditions
We threw out yesterday

God is crying
Torn up inside
Hoping his children
Can reach the other side

Without God's love in your life
No hope will be in sight
Pray for God's forgiveness
For all to receive this night

God is crying above
With tears of hope
Praying for our salvation
For knowledge to gain before revelation

Giving us love and peace
And his Holy Book
Praying that his children
Will not be overlooked

## PREREQUISITE COURSES

One of the biggest differences there will be when the Precious One returns the second time is that he won't be coming back to help sinners. The Precious One won't have time to try to save sinners; he will be coming to eliminate evil and reward the righteous. His mission will be to establish God's Kingdom. If we haven't passed the prerequisite courses, it will be too late during the End Times. The righteous that died before the End Times were freed from sin through death. Sin had no dominion over them for they were not under the law but under grace. Romans 6:17-18 reminds us, *"But God be thanked, that ye were the servants of sin, but ye have obeyed from the heart that form of doctrine which was delivered you. Being then made free from sin, ye became the servants of righteousness."* When the Precious One returns, the prerequisite courses must be passed, as we will need both advocates, Holy Spirit and the second Comforter, abiding in us.

### *PREREQUISITE COURSES:*

1. Love God with all your heart.
2. Love your neighbor as yourself.

    *"On these two commandments hang all the law and the prophets."* (Matthew 22:40)

3. Love one another as the Precious One has loved us.

    The third prerequisite course came from the Precious One: *"A new commandment I give unto you, That ye love one another; as I have loved you, that ye also love*

## Chapter 3: JUDGMENT DAY

*one another. By this shall all men know that ye are my disciples, if ye have love one to another."* (John 13:34-35)

The Precious One's commandment is the hardest one to pass! If we don't pass this commandment, we will not receive another Comforter which will abide in us forever. This second Comforter is from the Precious One and it is not given out so easily. When we pass our prerequisite courses and the Precious One sees that we are following his commandment he will ask the Father to send us the second Comforter. Receiving the second Comforter is requested of God by The Precious One, but whether it is received is a decision only God can make. Like a good Son, he has to ask the Father to grant his wish. If granted we will have the right blood flowing through us, the blood of the Precious One. He will never leave us comfortless! He will dwell in us and all our works will be good. John 14:12 promises, *"Verily, verily, I say unto you, He that believeth on me, the works that I do shall he do also; and greater works than these shall he do; because I go unto my Father."*

These are the prerequisite courses that we must pass. Our life will be reborn, and people will see our light shining so bright. It is critical that during the End Times we have the second Comforter in us. That Comforter is from the Precious One, but many will not receive it. The second Comforter teaches us all things and brings all things to our remembrance, whatsoever the Precious One says unto us. Understand that, *"there are three that bear record in heaven, the Father, the Word, and the Holy Ghost: and these three are one. And there are three that bear witness in earth, the Spirit, and the water, and the blood: and these three agree in one"* (I John 5:7-8).

The second Comforter is the Spirit of Truth who can only be given to us by the Precious One praying to God to send us the second Comforter which will abide with us forever:

> *And I will pray the Father, and he shall give you another Comforter, that he may abide with you for ever; Even the Spirit of truth; whom the world cannot receive, because it seeth him not, neither knoweth him: but ye know him; for he dwelleth with you, and shall be in you. I will not leave you comfortless: I will come to you. Yet a little while, and the world seeth me no more; but ye see me: because I live, ye shall live also. At that day ye shall know that I am in my Father, and ye in me, and I in you. He that hath my commandments, and keepeth them, he it is that loveth me: and he that loveth me shall be loved of my Father, and I will love him, and will manifest myself to him.*
> (John 14:16-21)

Understand that the Precious One knew his fate and destination, just as we will know our fate and destination if we fail the prerequisite courses. So we must pass the prerequisite courses, and then we will receive the second Comforter and the works will be easy! Here are some classes that will refresh our love for one another and prepare us for our works before Judgment Day.

## JUDGMENT DAY 101

CHARITY/LOVE/SURRENDER
PRAYER/WORSHIP/HOLINESS
FAITH/WORKS/DISCIPLESHIP

Chapter 3: JUDGMENT DAY

## ***CHARITY/LOVE/SURRENDER***

The Precious One said, *"Thou shalt love the Lord thy God with all thy heart, and with all thy soul, and with all thy mind. This is the first and great commandment. And the second is like unto it, Thou shalt love thy neighbour as thyself"* (Matthew 22:37-39).

I think the hardest thing to realize is that God knew us before we were here. We are no accident, and God loves us! We were created in his image. So first understand that we have a purpose and a mission for being here. When we realize that our life has a purpose from God, surrendering is easier and understandable. God loves us and he planned us for his purposes.

Ephesians 1:11 tells us this very thing: *"In whom also we have obtained an inheritance, being predestinated according to the purpose of him who worketh all things after the counsel of his own will."* Remember the words of Proverbs 3:5-6: *"Trust in the Lord with all thine heart; and lean not unto thine own understanding. In all thy ways acknowledge him, and he shall direct thy paths."* We can't serve our mission without surrendering our life to the Precious One. When we do that, we are like a reborn child, a child who surrenders their will, thoughts, plans, and emotions to the Precious One. When we surrender our life to him, it will lead us to a path which brings joy, peace, love, and happiness. We are now in the light.

Ephesians 5:8 exhorts us, *"For ye were sometimes darkness, but now are ye light in the Lord: walk as children of light."* And in John 8:12 we read, *"Then spake Jesus again unto them, saying, I am the light of the world: he that followeth me shall not walk in darkness, but shall have the light of life."* We must be totally committed to the Precious One. We must listen and be ready for whatever the Precious One tells us, as the second Comforter will guide us through any situation. The second Comforter is the only way to get the Precious One in our life. I believe that most people do love God and the Precious One, and as I stated before, I don't discount anyone's belief, but I strongly feel that most people don't love one another, and that is a prerequisite course that *must* be passed by the End Times.

If we look back at the 2008 and 2012 presidential election years, I'm sure we'd see that many people did not love their neighbor or one another. The hatred and racism were so apparent, but nobody wanted to call it what it was—racism at its highest level. Other nations seeing how we have treated the President of the USA can witness racism firsthand. This hatred and prejudice will keep many from receiving eternal life. Name-calling, calling him a liar, pointing the finger, disrespecting the President of the United States of America—I wonder what will happen when people actually meet the Judge. The Precious One probably can't wait to tell them, "I know you not."

The color of our skin will not even matter when we meet our maker. It was never about one religion or nationality or race being superior to another. I am amazed that people today still think that their race is superior to others. These attitudes will never get them through the gates of eternal life. The 100% believers always knew it was never about their race.

The ones belonging to the Superior Devil Shield Club forgot to remove their shields, because the war has been over. It was never about controlling, dictating, manipulating, mutilating, raping, or murdering others because they were different, whether it was over color, language, religion, territory, or culture. It was wrong—this attitude will never get them through the heavenly gates. When members of the Superior Devil Shield Club start to impose their attitudes or beliefs on others, it is wrong. The membership is dying but in groups the club feels empowered. The members of this slowing-dying club don't have the right to judge others. This club has been gathering members of all nationalities, as they have a common purpose. When we start seeing and hearing about the devilish destruction they cause around the world, understand it's their evil side emerging. In the United States of America, we have the right to protest peacefully and remove some of the members from the Superior Devil Shield Club by voting.

Voting is our right, and we elect people to do our will. If the leaders aren't for the people, vote them out. If we don't vote them out, just watch as their evil side will show its strong devilish presence. Understand it is not about their party, it's about their evil side, because evil has taken over their minds. The Devil is in control and we had better stand up against the devils, letting them know that having power, status, wealth, or a strong ego will never get them through the gates of eternal life.

I am amazed that certain people are still fighting the Affordable Care Act. Healthcare is for the good of the people. The parties couldn't even work together to make it better. The ACA is like a blueprint plan—as a contractor finishes the project he submits change orders to make it better. We have never submitted change orders to make the ACA better. We are fighting for healthcare coverage for many, but a few are trying to destroy it. Is it that they don't like it because a Black President signed the bill, doing the will of the people? Or don't they care about the masses of the people in the USA that had no health insurance coverage? If the devils are successful in destroying ACA, what alternative is there to having affordable health care for the masses of Americans?

The members of this club will never pass the prerequisite courses, because two of the prerequisite courses are about loving others—love thy neighbor and love one another. Many people are too jealous, envious, racist and straight-out hateful to love others, and they aren't hiding it anymore! We need to wake up as the Superior Devil Shield Club is getting active and recruiting more members, and they come in all colors.

Remember this from Chapter 1, "Devil's Heaven":

> *Now the works of the flesh are manifest, which are these; Adultery, fornication, uncleanness, lasciviousness, idolatry, witchcraft, hatred, variance, emulations, wrath, strife, seditions, heresies, envyings, murders, drunkenness, revellings, and such like: of the which I tell you in time past, that they which do such things shall not inherit the kingdom of God.* (Galatians 5:19-21)

Now 50% believers, or those belonging to the Superior Devil Shield Club who don't want to repent, are excluded from this class, Judgment Day 101. They couldn't pass the most important step. Therefore they can skip this chapter and continue reading Chapter IV. With no charity and love in their hearts they will never surrender their lives to the Precious One, and he will never ask God to give them his Comforter. Hopeless souls, their destinations are already plotted.

Chapter 3: JUDGMENT DAY

**PRAYER/WORSHIP/HOLINESS**

The Precious One said:
> And when thou prayest, thou shalt not be as the hypocrites are: for they love to pray standing in the synagogues and in the corners of the streets, that they may be seen of men. Verily I say unto you, They have their reward. But thou, when thou prayest, enter into thy closet, and when thou hast shut thy door, pray to thy Father which is in secret; and thy Father which seeth in secret shall reward thee openly. But when ye pray, use not vain repetitions, as the heathen do: for they think that they shall be heard for their much speaking. Be not ye therefore like unto them: for your Father knoweth what things ye have need of, before ye ask him. After this manner therefore pray ye: Our Father which art in heaven, Hallowed be thy name. Thy kingdom come. Thy will be done in earth, as it is in heaven. Give us this day our daily bread. And forgive us our debts, as we forgive our debtors. And lead us not into temptation, but deliver us from evil: For thine is the kingdom, and the power, and the glory, for ever. Amen. (Matthew 6:5-13)

When we pray, what an intimate relationship we will have with God! We will have the ability to hear his response to us. When we pray and want a talk with God, we will know when God is talking to *us*. Spending time with God in prayer is a high priority, wanting to listen and hear what God wants to tell us. Having a little talk with God is such a great blessing!

In Luke 11:28 Jesus speaks to us, *"But he said, Yea rather, blessed are they that hear the word of God, and keep it."* Everybody needs their own personal relationship with God. We need to be consistent with our worship to him. Above all be ourselves, be genuine, unique, and authentic when we pray and worship God with love. Having a sacred and holy relationship with God and offering him absolute adoration and reverence is the purist praise and worship that we can give. Remember, God created us in his image and he loves us, and we need to thank him, worship him, praise him, glorify him, pray to him, and love him every day of our existence!

Listening and praying go hand in hand. When we talk to God, we need to listen for the response. The Holy Spirit will talk to us. It may not be what we expected, but God does know best. Many believers will give up waiting for a response to their need, but just make sure it's a need and not a want! Taking the time to have an intimate worship and prayer moment with God is the revelation of holiness, it transforms the carnal mind to a spiritual mind. Holiness makes it easy to humble ourselves and have a deep, personal, spiritual relationship with God. The Holy Spirit is on fire. That special time is so important. Staying in Devil's Heaven prevents this time of oneness. Decisions must be made, because we can't have it both ways—God's or the Devil's, a choice must be made. The Seal of God or the Mark of the Beast—it is very simple and straightforward for the believer.

Chapter 3: JUDGMENT DAY

### **FAITH/WORKS/DISCIPLESHIP**

*"And Jesus came and spake unto them, saying, All power is given unto me in heaven and in earth. Go ye therefore, and teach all nations, baptizing them in the name of the Father, and of the Son, and of the Holy Ghost: Teaching them to observe all things whatsoever I have commanded you: and, lo, I am with you always, even unto the end of the world. Amen"* (Matthew 28:18-20). We should know by now that we have a purpose and mission and that surrendering our life to the Precious One should not be an issue. Through prayer and worship, what an intimate relationship we will have with the Precious One, knowing the works that must be done. Our task is now works and discipleship. Ultimate achievement! Giving service to others and spreading the Good News!

The Precious One told his disciples, *"Go ye into all the world, and preach the gospel to every creature. He that believeth and is baptized shall be saved; but he that believeth not shall be damned"* (Mark 16:15-16). When we have the light burning bright within ourselves there is no stopping us from spreading the Good News and doing the works of the Precious One. Doing his works should be a natural process. Spreading the news of how God has blessed us should not be hard. How and where we start discipleship has always been a part of our own trials and tribulations. It can start with our testimonials, telling others how God has healed us and how his glory and light shine so bright. We need to be telling our testimonials to others so they can see the light in us and know that we give all praises to God.

I remember when I suffered a stroke at my family reunion in 2009 while talking to my Aunt. I instantly went into prayer and asked God that his will be done. After praying I was able to walk up the hill and sit down by my cousin. I told her that I had a stroke. While driving me to the hospital she asked whether I wanted to go to Kaiser or Mercy Methodist Hospital. I told her Mercy Methodist Hospital. Walking in to emergency I knew what to expect—long waiting lines. That Saturday night after 8 pm there was no one waiting in line but me! That was a miracle on a Saturday night with no one in the emergency room but me. God is good!

Once the MRI was completed and the doctor told me I had suffered a stroke, he was amazed that the only problem I still had was numbness in my lips. The stroke hit me on the right cerebral hemisphere of the brain and affected my left side. The next morning the doctors did an ultrasound and a CAT scan. Noticing that the doctors were discussing me, I asked them to tell me what was on their minds. One doctor said, "You have no blood flowing on your right side to the brain." I told them that is correct, as I had an aneurysm in 2000 and the doctor had placed two balloons cutting the blood flow from my right carotid artery to my brain.

Then the doctors huddled and talked to each other, forgetting the patient, me. I asked what was going on. They informed me that if the stroke had been on my left side I would be dead or very handicapped. I told them that I served a good God and that I hadn't finished my mission for him. I just had a wake-up call and I knew what I had to do. God answers prayers, and through all the trials and tribulations that I endured, I kept on believing in God and with my faith there was nothing I couldn't handle!

This is a true testimony and if I don't tell others my testimonies, I do a disservice to God. God protected me from the beginning of the stroke to the end. God protected me from the beginning of the aneurysm to the end. God is protecting me

## Chapter 3: JUDGMENT DAY

now. I know who my protector is. Tell your stories, pass the prerequisite courses and do good works so the Precious One will ask God to send you the second Comforter. I know that my light shines bright as the second Comforter abides in me. I needed the Precious One's blood to be counted.

### *Rise Up & Be Counted*

Rise up & Be Counted
All God's children
Must be in place
Time draws near
Let's make no mistakes

Rise Up & Be Counted
God's seal is upon us
Dying for the cause
God's reward
Will find us all

Rise Up & Be Counted
When the Savior comes
Stand high & bow down
To the blessed
And anointed one

Rise Up & Be Counted
No one could turn our faith
Antichrist & False Prophet
Bottomless pit
Your destiny waits

Rise Up & Be Counted
For our blessing to receive
The seal of God
Is all that we need
Press forward on to victory

Rise Up & Be Counted
Never doubting the truth
Believing in our Savior
Praying, praying
But getting us through

Rise Up & Be Counted
Shout and claim victory
Peace, love & eternal life
Oh! What a blessing
Having the second Comforter in our life

Rise Up & Be Counted
Glory be to our Father above
Obedient believers
Fought the battle on our knees
Faithful through it all

## WORKS

With hatred and racism on the rise, Judgment Day will be quick and easy for the Precious One—pass or fail. Does it make us feel saved by raising our hands and vocalizing the phrase, "I do accept the Precious One as my personal Lord and Savior"? James 2:14 says, *"What doth it profit, my brethren, though a man say he hath faith, and have not works? can faith save him?"* Con-

## Chapter 3: JUDGMENT DAY

tinuing, James 2:17 states, *"Even so faith, if it hath not works, is dead, being alone."* He concludes in James 2:26, *"For as the body without the spirit is dead, so faith without works is dead also."*

Though faith is necessary to be saved, it takes more than faith. I believe that "works" has been erased or forgotten from many people's minds. The works of the Precious One must be carried out, not forgotten. The 100% believers are doing the works of the Precious One. Don't become complacent and let the hole in Devil's Heaven continue to grow, surrounding us with sin that we haven't repented from. As believers, we know what's right or wrong. The Precious One wants sinners to repent from their sins before he returns.

If we have a very prosperous life, but continue to sin, are our blessings coming from God or Satan? That is why I explained at the beginning that I didn't take away from anyone's faith. We can *tell* anybody that we believe, but understand that 100% believers can't be fooled—their works tell a different story and *they* can see that the light isn't shining in the 50% believers. Unfortunately, many aren't listening to the Holy Spirit, and the Precious One will not pray to God to give the 50% believers the second Comforter. Listening to the Holy Spirit will guide us right, and I do believe that God is trying to bless us. After awhile, if we are still in Devil's Heaven, I believe it will be time for God to place us on the back burner, letting us deal with our decisions and the repercussions. The Holy Spirit needs to take time out as we foolishly enjoy being 50% believers in Devil's Heaven. Without repentance for our sins the Devil has won.

The Devil is constantly trying to destroy families and marriages. That crafty Devil doesn't have to win. It's time to take a proactive stand against the Devil! We have a lot of work to do. Sit back and start our list. Satan's master plan is making mere believers believe they are saved. We have become a materialistic world and have forgotten that we must walk not after the flesh, but after the Spirit. Is your light shining or has it been blown out? Matthew 5:16 says, *"Let your light so shine before men, that they may see your good works, and glorify your Father which is in heaven."*

We need a boycott! We have accepted sin and lust as the standard. We have become so complacent that if we don't boycott, many will not be saved. Nobody wants to go against the grain—that's not popular! We have got to boycott and take a proactive stance against the norm. It's going to be hard because Satan has let us think that everything is okay. It's not! We have to get back to the basics and the teachings of God and the Precious One. The chosen generation has been called out of darkness into the light, the 100% believers, but the Devil loves to keep the 50% believers in the darkness.

Receiving blessings from God or blessings from Satan is our choice. We can't serve Satan and be saved. We have allowed Satan's master plan into our lives. Devil's Heaven believers are not saved—in reality they are so lost! We have looked the other way and justified our sins. They have justified wrong. The Precious One said in Matthew 4:10, *"Get thee hence, Satan: for it is written, Thou shalt worship the Lord thy God, and him only shalt thou serve."* The hole of Devil's Heaven is so big that Satan has blinded many from the truth. Many will think they are saved, but remember, eternity is too long to be wrong.

In John 14:12-16, Jesus says, *"Verily, verily, I say unto you,*

## Chapter 3: JUDGMENT DAY

*He that believeth on me, the works that I do shall he do also; and greater works than these shall he do; because I go unto my Father. And whatsoever ye shall ask in my name, that will I do, that the Father may be glorified in the Son. If ye shall ask any thing in my name, I will do it. If ye love me, keep my commandments. And I will pray the Father, and he shall give you another Comforter, that he may abide with you for ever."* Is the second Comforter abiding in us? It is not God's plan for us to die and not have everlasting life, for God loves us. We need to repent from the slavery to sin and lust before Judgment Day. The Precious One is coming back as Judge! What will the Precious One say to us?

### Judgment Day

When I see you
What will you say?
My head will drop low
A sign of guilt
It will betray
Realization of what's to come
On my Judgment Day

Too late
Stepping back in time
To correct a sinful life
That I left behind
Didn't repent, even though
With faith, I believed in you
Saved and blessed
That's for you
To put me to the test

> Had plenty of chances
> To do the right thing
> Greed, sex, money, lust
> Just couldn't get enough
> Can't change what I did
> Disrespecting your rules
> And changing some too
>
> Though you are my Savior
> I may have to pay
> A price so high
> That I overlooked
> The miracle in you
> A blessing sent from high
> Faith and works, left behind
> On my Judgment Day

When Judgment Day comes our faith and works will be put to the test! It's time to close our hole and be accountable for our actions. Blessings from Satan are being distributed too easily. It's more serious than we think. God is a good, loving, and compassionate God, but he is also a God of wrath. Our sin is growing so abundantly that sometimes it's hard to continue to do the right thing. Satan has so exploited our minds that many are accepting the most blatant acts of sin.

The wickedness of man is strong today, and I thank God that he gave us the Precious One. Are we starting to understand why our hole is getting bigger? God will not destroy all living creatures on earth again. The wickedness of man is still with us, but God has always had a plan to deal with man's sins. His plan was his Son, the Precious One. The Precious One gave us prerequisite courses. We must pass the prerequisite courses, so we will have a chance of receiving the second Comforter from God. We will have the right blood flowing through us and our works will be good!

As believers, have we forgotten what the Precious One did while on earth? Have we forgotten the Precious One's commandments, or are we picking and choosing the ones we like to remember? The Precious One gave us a plan by which we can be saved. He didn't leave this earth without a blueprint plan. We must surrender all to the Precious One. He wants us to have a personal relationship with God. Here are some of the things that the Precious One did:

- Prayed to the Father.
- Loved the Father and all others.
- Fed the people.
- Preached and taught the gospel of the kingdom.
- Healed all manner of sickness and disease among the people.
- Taught his disciples.
- Raised Lazarus from the grave.
- Healed a leper and made him clean.
- Healed Peter's wife's mother, sick with fever.
- Walked on water.
- Died for remission of our sins.

There are so many miracles that the Precious One did, but his greatest gift was dying on Calvary so we could have the chance to receive everlasting life. Seeing the Precious One working miracles, many people witnessed firsthand that he was different and unique. God knew that the Precious One's birth had to be a wake-up call to all, and his death and resurrection had to be the solution to it all. The Precious One knew what his mission was on Earth.

As believers, are we doing the righteous works of the Precious One? We constantly and knowingly continue to hurt people whom we love. We must replace our negative thoughts, deeds, and actions with positive works. Let's stand back, be still, and take a good look at our life histories. Do we love our neighbors and others? Can you see why we are sinking so fast and can't even see a way out of our situation? Stop and ask yourself if this was the plan God intended for his people. Most believers do understand why their hole is getting bigger—it's the consciousness that if we don't repent before Judgment Day it will be too late for eternal life. If we should die before Judgment Day without repentance for our sins, there will be no pass to heaven. Remember, God destroyed an entire wicked city of lust and sin.

We may need a wake-up call to understand just why our hole keeps expanding. We need to sincerely repent of our sins and let the Precious One abide in us. Do we just repeat history and continue our bad past experiences? Haven't we learned anything from past history taught in God's book? Even today people have forgotten God's love and replaced it with the Devil's agenda. The Precious One's commandment has been erased from the minds of those who are determined to destroy many, whose works are devilish on issues such as:

## Chapter 3: JUDGMENT DAY

- Healthcare
- Immigration
- Education
- Social Security
- Food stamps
- Medicaid expansion
- Voting rights
- Cost of living and fair wages

Anything that is for the people will always be opposed by certain factions. The problem for those in the Superior Devil Shield Club is that in the United States of America we have become a melting pot country, and the majority race has now become the minority race.

- They want to control and dictate, but not be told what to do.
- They want to be in first place—second place just won't do.
- They want to set policies and rules, while taking away our rights.
- They want to dictate and govern, while taking away the power of government.

The members of this Club have evil and hatred in their hearts—just imagine their Judgment Day! The Precious One will know them not. Just look at their faces—it is like staring into darkness, because it's clear they have no love for one another. I am saying this to stress how important it is for each of us to pass the prerequisite courses during the End Times. We all need to receive the second Comforter rewarded by God!

## JUDGMENT DAY

Judgment Day is real! Unfortunately, many people have darkness in their souls—their light doesn't shine. We are commissioned to preach, teach, and baptize people in the name of the Father, and of the Son, and of the Holy Ghost. While 50% believers are probably good people, their weakness allows the Devil to be in control, and without repentance our lives will be over on Judgment Day. If the Devil has invaded our minds, souls, and bodies we aren't thinking rationally. It is time to take control of our lives before we lose them. The Precious One will not give us a pass into eternal life—we must repent and do the right things.

We must go through the Precious One to get to God, nothing else is acceptable. The righteous life is the only way to live, because the Precious One is returning to judge everyone. It makes perfect sense for the Precious One to judge us. He died for the remission of sin, so who is better to judge us than he, the perfect Son born into a sinful world and dying without sin. When the Precious One was resurrected and ascended to God, he had accomplished half his mission. He will return to complete the second half. God

## Chapter 3: JUDGMENT DAY

has given him the power to judge the world. He will defeat Satan and judge all mankind.

Time is running out for lost souls, and we are either in or out! Faith without works is dead. Faith and works go hand in hand. I was once in church when the pastor preached on the topic, "Do you look like your Father?" Thinking about that, I realized that when people meet us we should be asking ourselves, "Do they see my Father in me?" Is the light shining so bright that people see that you look like your Father? We were created in God's image and we must be about his work. Looking in the mirror, can we see whether our father is God or Satan?

On Judgment Day it will be easy for the Precious One to judge us, as most will already know their outcome. It will all be about our life on earth, and we won't be able to undo what we did. On Judgment Day we don't get three strikes—the history of our life will already be written. No lies or strange stories can we tell. Our life's book is open on Judgment Day and it can't be rewritten. Our character will already have been judged. While even we can tell a lot about a person's character, the Precious One will know whether it's light or darkness in our souls by *instantly* analyzing our characters. Webster's II New Riverside Desk Dictionary has this definition:

### character
1. A distinguishing feature; characteristic
2. The group of ethical and mental characteristics that mark a person or group
3. Moral integrity
4. Reputation
5. *(Informal)* An eccentric person

In Josephson Institute's Center for Youth Ethics they discuss the Six Pillars of Character. (http://charactercounts.org/sixpillars.html):

1. Trustworthiness
   Be honest—Don't deceive, cheat, or steal—Be reliable—Do what you say you'll do—Have the courage to do the right thing—Build a good reputation—Be loyal—Stand by your family, friends, and country

2. Respect
   Treat others with respect; follow the Golden Rule—Be tolerant and accepting of differences—Use good manners, not bad language—Be considerate of the feelings of others—Don't threaten, hit or hurt anyone—Deal peacefully with anger, insults, and disagreements

3. Responsibility
   Do what you are supposed to do—Plan ahead—Persevere: keep on trying!—Always do your best—Use self-control—Be self-disciplined—Think before you act—Consider the consequences—Be accountable for your words, actions, and attitudes—Set a good example for others

4. Fairness
   Play by the rules—Take turns and share—Be open-minded; listen to others—Don't blame others carelessly—Treat all people fairly

5. Caring
   Be kind—Be compassionate and show you care—Express gratitude—Forgive others—Help people in need

## Chapter 3: JUDGMENT DAY

6. Citizenship
Do your share to make school and community better—Cooperate—Get involved in community affairs—Stay informed; vote—Be a good neighbor—Obey laws and rules—Respect authority—Protect the environment—Volunteer

Considering the above Six Pillars of Character, we can see that it will be an easy job for the Precious One on Judgment Day. It will not be a guessing game, just the facts, and the facts of our character that we wrote in our lifetime. The Precious One will know our destiny—either in light or darkness—when he sees us on Judgment Day. The Precious One is not coming back to convince us to be saved and to repent of our sin. He will be here to judge—that is his only mission on Judgment Day. Don't think receiving eternal life is a slam dunk! I've stated that we do have time to pass the prerequisite courses before Judgment Day. God is giving us time to pass them!

The next three chapters will give us a time line as to when the Precious One will return:  Chapter 4: Sounding Trumpets; Chapter 5: Mark of the Beast; and Chapter 6: End Time Witnesses. Listed below are some of the events that will be taking place during the sounding of the Sixth Trumpet. The time to pass the prerequisite courses is during the sounding of the Sixth Trumpet, and many believe that the Sixth Trumpet has already sounded! During the Sixth Trumpet the following events will take place:

- Two billion humans will die in WWIII.
- The Antichrist and False Prophet will emerge.
- The third temple will be built in Jerusalem and the Antichrist will desecrate it.

- The Mark of the Beast will be implemented.
- Two End Time Witnesses will preach for 3½ years.

Once the two End Time Witnesses are killed by the Antichrist, our time to pass the prerequisite courses will be over—the Seventh Trumpet will sound and the Precious One will return. The following three chapters will explain that God has allowed us time to pass the prerequisite courses. We need to pass these prerequisite courses, so our works will be apparent to others. They will see our light shining so bright and know that we have received the second Comforter prayed by the Precious One and that we have been rewarded by God.

Chapter 4

# SOUNDING TRUMPETS
## *Good and Evil: God's action plan*

The exact time of the Precious One's return is unknown. As the prophecy in Matthew 24:36 states, *"But of that day and hour knoweth no man, no, not the angels of heaven, but my Father only."* We need to be ready. We may not know the exact time of the Precious One's return but we know He *will* return. There will be many signs marking the season of his return. The signs are everywhere. Every time we listen or watch the news on the TV, Internet or radio the signs are very apparent. Signs that have happened in all generations now come to pass more frequently —earthquakes, thunderstorms, hurricanes, tornados, mudslides, avalanches, and tsunamis. Terrorism, which has always been here, is now prompting the USA to become a major player in the effort to end it through warfare. The signs are here!

God is giving us many signs that the Precious One will return to earth. All the signs are events that we have no imminent control over. God does not tell us the time of the Precious One's return, because that would defeat the purpose. The 50% believers would stay in sin just until the time for the Precious One's return if they knew the year, month, and day! God wants the 50% believers to repent *now* and not wait for the Precious One's return. It will be too late to repent when he comes back. God wants His people to be saved, but he wants us to make a decision between his Son and Satan.

While God has given and will give us many signs to let us know he's in charge, we still want more proof! God has given us proof but our eyes just haven't been open to see it. God has always had his action plan in place. God, the Almighty Father, is implementing the end of man's rule and governance on earth once and for all. Understand that God has given us warnings to let us know that the Precious One is coming soon and that if we don't pass the prerequisite courses it will be too late for us to be saved. The warning signs already should have awakened us to the truth that God's master plan has always been in effect. God has always given us a road map to the Precious One's return. Let's take a look at the warning signs. We have three categories of warnings:

1. Minor warnings
2. Major warnings
3. Final warnings

## WARNING SIGNS

### *MINOR WARNINGS*

The minor warnings have been here for centuries:
- Wars and rumors of war
- Nations rising against nations, kingdoms against kingdoms
- Famines, pestilences , hunger

## Chapter 4: SOUNDING TRUMPETS

- Plagues
- Earthquakes, tsunamis, storms, hurricanes, tornados, volcanic eruptions
- Terrorist attacks
- Changes in the weather (fall looking like summer, etc.)
- False prophets/antichrists arising and deceiving many
- Men lovers of themselves
- Children disobedient to parents
- Traitors
- Lovers of pleasure rather than lovers of God
- People unthankful and unholy
- Heavy sinners and driven by lust
- Adultery, fornication, murders, witchcraft

These are just minor warnings and yet people haven't repented of their sins or realized that the Precious One will return and judge each of us! They don't believe 100%, and Satan has twisted their minds. The minor warnings will never go away—they are our wake-up call to make sure we know that the Precious One will return and that God is in control. God is giving humans many chances for eternal life, yet souls are still being deceived by Satan. God had to put more heat to the fire with major warnings like the Seven Sounding Trumpets.

### **MAJOR WARNINGS**

The Seven Trumpets are in the Bible in the book of Revelation. The First Trumpet sounds in Revelation 8:7 and continues until all seven trumpets have sounded. When a trumpet sounds it announces something major, so the announcement had to be about major events. I believe the Seven Sounding Trumpets are about the following:

1. Trumpet #1—World War I, Joseph Stalin and Adolf Hitler's scorched-earth policy, 1914–1918; 1933–1945.
2. Trumpet #2—World War II, 1939–1945.
3. Trumpet #3—Chernobyl/Wormwood nuclear disaster, 4/26/1986.
4. Trumpet #4—Global warming, speeding up as the end approaches. This is midway for the trumpets, and the last three trumpets will sound faster than the first three trumpets.
5. Trumpet #5—Saddam Hussein and the Gulf War, 1990–1991.
6. Trumpet #6—Major World War III; Antichrist emerges; Mark of the Beast and End Time Witnesses.
7. Trumpet #7—Final battle between the Precious One and the Antichrist at Armageddon.

Let's discuss the first five sounding trumpets. Many believe that they have already sounded and their events have taken place.

## 1–5 SOUNDING TRUMPETS
### Trumpet #1

Revelation 8:7:
> *The first angel sounded, and there followed hail and fire mingled with blood, and they were cast upon the earth: and the third part of trees was burnt up, and all green grass was burnt up.*

## Chapter 4: SOUNDING TRUMPETS

Many believe the First Trumpet to be World War I. Irvin Baxter, *Endtime Magazine*, March/April 2009, featured the cover story, "World Government…Forming Now!" Article under Letters & Feedback states, *"Possibly World War I. During this trumpet, John described hail and fire mingled with blood being cast to the earth. During WWI, for the first time in the history of warfare, airplanes were used to drop bombs on the armies below. John described the resulting devastation as hail and fire, mingled with blood. The prophecy also states that the third part of the trees and the grass was burned up. During World War I, the armies commonly employed a tactic called the 'scorched earth policy.' The purpose was to deny the enemy access to crops and shelter needed to sustain their forces."*

The effects of the war included many barren tracts of land along the Western Front. Flamethrowers, which terrorized the French and British soldiers, were used by the German army in the early stages of WWI. The main purpose of the flamethrower is to spread fire by launching burning fuel. The prophecy states that the third part of the trees and the grass was burned up. The flamethrower denied the enemy access to necessities needed to sustain their forces. Adolf Hitler had scorched-earth policies that left cities and towns devastated.

I believe we must also include the Holocaust within John's vision. Hail and fire mingled with blood—this could be a vision of the six million Jews who lost their lives under Adolf Hitler and the Nazi Party (National Socialist German Workers' Party) from 1933 to 1945. The Nazi party wanted to terminate all races they considered inferior. Holocaust is derived from the Greek words meaning "completely burnt." Ken Raggio, in his article, "The Seven Trumpets of Revelation," writes, "Joseph Stalin was at first terrified by Adolph Hitler, and sent hordes of bomb squads to enact a 'scorched earth policy' on the Ukraine in 1941, to drive back Hitler's invasion. The Ukraine was left in utter devastation." He continues, "Incidentally, for what it's worth, this First Trumpet accompanies the historical extermination of SIX MILLION JEWS by Adolph Hitler, AND it occurs immediately before the founding of the MODERN STATE OF ISRAEL. These co-incidents beg consideration as a message from God Almighty." Neither of these antichrists cared about their neighbors, because they saw themselves as dictators. Noncompliance with their programs meant death to the traitors. WWI killed millions of people and left millions prisoners or missing in action. The First Trumpet is over.

**Trumpet #2**

Revelation 8:8-9:
> *And the second angel sounded, and as it were a great mountain burning with fire was cast into the sea: and the third part of the sea became blood; And the third part of the creatures which were in the sea, and had life, died; and the third part of the ships were destroyed.*

Many believe this to be World War II. This war started in 1939 and ended in 1945. WWII involved major world powers in a war for global control—seven long years of a war of wars. "There were approximately 105,000 ships in WWII and over 36,000 of those were destroyed in battle - almost EXACTLY one-third of the ships! WWII is certainly remembered for its spectacular sea battles, beginning at Pearl Harbor. Another prophesy fulfilled!" (Ken Raggio, "The Seven Trumpets of Revelation"). John's vision

## Chapter 4: SOUNDING TRUMPETS

in Revelation was very graphic and he could have been describing the atomic bomb. Irvin Baxter writes, *"Furthermore, John saw a great mountain burning with fire cast into the sea. Does an atomic mushroom cloud resemble a mountain burning with fire? Absolutely! The first and only atomic bombs in all of history were dropped on Hiroshima and Nagasaki, Japan at the close of WWII. Were they cast into the sea? Yes. Japan is a series of 3,000 islands in the sea. John had obviously never seen an atomic explosion, but that is exactly what he described.* ("World Government...Forming Now!," March/April 2009. Article under Letters & Feedback).

Not only did the atomic bomb take human lives, it killed the creatures of the sea, too. The atomic bombing of Hiroshima and Nagasaki ended the war in the Pacific with the surrender of Japan. President Truman's decision to use this catastrophic nuclear device opened up a dangerous area, the nuclear arms race. WWII was devastating, with strong antichrists in control. Their soldiers or citizens did as instructed, with no compassion for mankind, only brutal dictatorship. The Second Trumpet is over.

### Trumpet #3

Revelation 8:10-11:
> *And the third angel sounded, and there fell a great star from heaven, burning as it were a lamp, and it fell upon the third part of the rivers, and upon the fountains of waters; And the name of the star is called Wormwood: and the third part of the waters became wormwood; and many men died of the waters, because they were made bitter.*

I believe the Third Trumpet to be the devastating explosion at the Chernobyl nuclear plant. Irvin Baxter's *Endtime Magazine* cover story "World Government Forming Now!" continues: "*The Ukrainian word for wormwood is Chernobyl. On April 26, 1986, a nuclear power plant named Chernobyl located near Pripyat, Ukraine, exploded, shooting radiation one mile into the sky. A storm system absorbed the radiation and traveled across Europe, raining nuclear contaminated precipitation into the soil and bodies of water. Verse 11 reveals that many men died of the waters. This is exactly what happened with Chernobyl. Over 125,000 have died and still counting.*" In addition to the many lives taken, those that survived the explosion could turn up with sickness many years later. Ken Raggio, in his article, "The Seven Trumpets of Revelation," says, "*The Russian word, "Chernobyl," means "Wormwood," as mentioned in these verses. It certainly appears that the third trumpet sounded on April 26, 1986. In Chernobyl, Ukraine, the worst nuclear accident in history exposed 6.6 million people to potentially lethal radiation, contaminating the Dnieper River and reservoir, one of Europe's largest water systems. GREENPEACE claims that 200,000 premature deaths have already occurred, and predicts 270,000 more cancer cases. Countless others will eventually suffer disease and premature deaths.*" The Third Trumpet is over.

### Trumpet #4

Revelation 8:12:
> *And the fourth angel sounded, and the third part of the sun was smitten, and the third part of the moon, and the third part of the stars; so as the third part of them was darkened, and the day shone not for a third part of it, and the night likewise.*

## Chapter 4: SOUNDING TRUMPETS

I believe the Fourth Trumpet is about global dimming and the fact that God is speeding up the last three trumpets. Ken Raggio in his article, "The Seven Trumpets of Revelation," continues, saying, "*Consider this article from the New York Times, 5/13/04: 'Globe Grows Darker as Sunshine Diminishes 10% to 37%.' In the second half of the 20th century, the world became, quite literally, a darker place. Defying expectation and easy explanation, hundreds of instruments around the world recorded a drop in sunshine reaching the surface of Earth, as much as 10 percent from the late 1950s to the early 90s, or 2 percent to 3 percent a decade. In some regions like Asia, the United States and Europe, the drop was steeper. In Hong Kong, sunlight decreased 37 percent. Dr. James E. Hansen, director of the NASA Goddard Institute for Space Studies in Manhattan, said that scientists had long known that pollution particles reflected some sunlight, but that they were now realizing the magnitude of the effect. So in certain places, the earth is already 1/3 darker, both day and night.*"

I would add that God is also telling us that the last three trumpets will occur faster than the first three sounding trumpets. That time has already sped up, as I believe we are in the Sixth Trumpet and it is now 2015. God is in control and has always been in control. The Fourth Trumpet was the halfway point and God is speeding up the timing of events on His plan, not man's. In Matthew 24:29-34 we read:

> *Immediately after the tribulation of those days shall the sun be darkened, and the moon shall not give her light, and the stars shall fall from heaven, and the powers of the heavens shall be shaken: And then shall appear the sign of the Son of man in heaven: and then*

shall all the tribes of the earth mourn, and they shall see the Son of man coming in the clouds of heaven with power and great glory. And he shall send his angels with a great sound of a trumpet, and they shall gather together his elect from the four winds, from one end of heaven to the other. Now learn a parable of the fig tree; When his branch is yet tender, and putteth forth leaves, ye know that summer is nigh: So likewise ye, when ye shall see all these things, know that it is near, even at the doors. Verily I say unto you, This generation shall not pass, till all these things be fulfilled.

Please understand that time is becoming shorter! The hourglass is running out of sand and those that haven't repented of their sins will be forgotten souls. Wake up and repent now! The Fourth Trumpet is over.

**Trumpet #5**

Revelation 9:1-12:
*And the fifth angel sounded, and I saw a star fall from heaven unto the earth: and to him was given the key of the bottomless pit. And he opened the bottomless pit; and there arose a smoke out of the pit, as the smoke of a great furnace; and the sun and the air were darkened by reason of the smoke of the pit. And there came out of the smoke locusts upon the earth: and unto them was given power, as the scorpions of the earth have power. And it was commanded them that they should not hurt the grass of the earth, neither any green thing, neither any tree; but only those men*

## Chapter 4: SOUNDING TRUMPETS

*which have not the seal of God in their foreheads. And to them it was given that they should not kill them, but that they should be tormented five months: and their torment was as the torment of a scorpion, when he striketh a man. And in those days shall men seek death, and shall not find it; and shall desire to die, and death shall flee from them. And the shapes of the locusts were like unto horses prepared unto battle; and on their heads were as it were crowns like gold, and their faces were as the faces of men. And they had hair as the hair of women, and their teeth were as the teeth of lions. And they had breastplates, as it were breastplates of iron; and the sound of their wings was as the sound of chariots of many horses running to battle. And they had tails like unto scorpions, and there were stings in their tails: and their power was to hurt men five months. And they had a king over them, which is the angel of the bottomless pit, whose name in the Hebrew tongue is Abaddon, but in the Greek tongue hath his name Apollyon. One woe is past; and, behold, there come two woes more hereafter.*

Most people believe this Fifth Trumpet was the Gulf War, 1990-1991. Irvin Baxter, in his cover story, "World Government…Forming Now!" comments, "When Saddam Hussein was forced to withdraw from Kuwait in 1991, he set 700 of the world's oil wells on fire in retaliation. The sun and the sky were not seen over Kuwait for the next several months. In his vision, John saw what he described as locusts with breastplates of iron coming out of the smoke. He said locusts had faces like men and hair like women. Was John seeing jet airplanes with the faces of men in the cockpits? Did he see the smoke trails following the airplanes, describing those as having hair like women? John said that the sound of their wings was as the sound of many chariots going to battle. If you were seeing a jet airplane or a helicopter for the first time, how would you describe it? Even more remarkable is the name of the king that was over these forces. Verse 11 says they had a king over them called in Hebrew Abaddon, but in Greek Apollyon. Both of these names mean 'the destroyer.' The name Saddam is Arabic for destroyer. Is all of this mere coincidence? You decide."

Ken Raggio's article "The Seven Trumpets of Revelation" agrees and says, "*Moreover, their LEADER was named APOLLYON in the Greek language, and ABADDON in the Hebrew language. Those names mean "THE DESTROYER." Amazingly, the name SADDAM means "the destroyer." That fact was specifically offered by an elderly lady who was the midwife who delivered SADDAM Hussein at his birth, and recalled that Saddam's mother named him 'destroyer' because she had such a difficult time delivering him.*" The Fifth Trumpet is over.

We are living in a world that will not get better. It is not promised to get better. The world is being orchestrated for the final music of the end. In reviewing the First through Fifth Trumpets, I wanted to add a different twist to the blueprint plans to show us how strong the antichrists, dictators, leaders and rulers have been during the sounding of these trumpets. Regarding the sounding trumpets, while many may have different ideas about the events involved, most agree that it was necessary for them to be very major events in order to wake up the world. Whether these specific events are the correct ones or not, there can be no doubt that God has a blueprint plan for the Precious One's return. When each trumpet sounded it was a wake-up call to the world! God has always been in control and he is the Alpha and Omega of His history. Remember, it is God's history that is happening!

## KILLERS

I want your ears to hear and your eyes to read a different angle about the sounding trumpets. This book is about the Precious One returning to judge all, so we must realize that he has to battle the evil one, the Antichrist. I want the world to understand how simple it is to be under the dictatorship of one ruler and abide by his rules. With most dictators, if we don't go along with their rules, death seems to be the only alternative. We have had so many antichrists during the Sounding Trumpets that I couldn't name them all! Each dictator had the Devil in his heart, mind, body, and soul, with no room for God to penetrate. As we will see from the sounding of the Sixth Trumpet, another Antichrist will emerge who will have more power than any other. No prior antichrist will ever compare to what the final Antichrist will be like. The final Antichrist will be a smooth operator with Satan in the driver's seat! Some of the past antichrists will have nothing to compare to the final Antichrist. Adolf Hitler, Joseph Stalin, Mao Zedong (Mao Tse-tung), Saddam Hussein, Osama bin Laden, Jim Jones, and many others can't compare to the final Antichrist. This Antichrist will emerge with the sounding of the Sixth Trumpet and do miracles that will persuade most people to believe he is God. He will be a devil deceiver and ruthless to the bones. Antichrists have ruled the world for centuries, but the final Antichrist will be defeated by the Precious One.

An article called "Reflections on Killers" (www.moreorless.net.au/killers/reflections), states the following:

> *Killers often rise to the top, but to do so they need a polluted environment. Corruption of the political, corporate or social systems can create the conditions in which killers thrive. Once in power they are ruthless and difficult to remove.*
>
> *Killers often believe they are working for a greater social good, and in many cases their initial motivation and actions appear to bear this out.*
>
> *Romania's Nicolae Ceausescu began his political career fighting fascists during the Second World War and in the initial years of his dictatorship appeared to be steering his country to independence and prosperity. Indonesia's Suharto was successful in holding together his highly diverse and factious nation at a particularly vulnerable time. Even Adolf Hitler's regime initially brought stability to a society in danger of complete collapse.*
>
> *But such killers always foul their achievement with the toll of their excess.*
>
> *Other killers can only be described as purely bad – self serving, ignorant and corrupt. Uganda's Idi Amin did nothing for his country except inflict terror and*

## Chapter 4: SOUNDING TRUMPETS

*destruction. Efrain Rios Montt, Guatemala's Bible-bashing despot, was just another in that country's long line of murderous presidents. Burma's Ne Win and his cohorts turned a country full of promise into one of the world's most downtrodden and poor.*

*A common trait of all killers featured here is their unwavering belief in the rightness of their acts, if not those acts' complete righteousness. None of those who are now dead went to their graves with any sense of guilt or regret, and it is unlikely that any of those still living will. World-class killers are always loaded with hubris; an overweening belief in their own infallibility. They are paternalistic and proud. It is no coincidence that they are all men, just as it is no coincidence that they scorn democracy.*

*The extent to which killers are products or reflections of their societies should also not be overlooked. Just as heroes are icons of movements for social justice, killers are a distillation of the darkness on the outskirts of society that at times of stress seeps to the core.*

*Adolf Hitler was a master at playing on the underlying anti-Semitism that was endemic in Germany between the world wars. Serbia's Slobodan Milosevic never hesitated to exploit the historic distrust between the populations of Croats, Serbs, Muslims and Christians in Yugoslavia. Japan's Prince Yasuhiko Asaka was a symbol of the havoc that can be wrought when imperialism and militarism converge.*

> *This site provides a personal selection of killers from the 20th Century. The facts are as accurate as could be determined from credible sources available on the internet and elsewhere. The interpretation is entirely personal. It always is.*

These past reflections on killers have more in common than is realized. They all belonged to the Superior Devil Shield Club and the club still has plenty of members! They had the power to get others to believe in their sick plans and to follow through with the murdering of thousands of innocent people. There is an absolute power and control that erases one's ability to even stand up to defend the truth. Their minds have been taken over by the Devil and the truth can't penetrate through the junk that clouds their judgment.

When the Devil has our minds, we must fight and believe that we can see the truth and get out of Devil's Heaven. That shifty and shady Devil must get off our backs and out of our minds. Right or wrong is the choice that must be made when the final Antichrist arises. This fence can't be straddled at all—our life is on the line! A life of heavenly bliss or a torment in hell, everyone is allowed to make their own decision.

Don't follow the rules of the Antichrist! God's rules and commandments will win out in the end, for the Precious One is coming back to set everything right. It is the Precious One's mission to defeat the evils of this world and to establish God's Kingdom. Understand that the Precious One is coming back to defeat a powerful Antichrist at the sound of the Seventh Trumpet, the End Times. The Antichrist will become apparent at the sounding of the Sixth Trumpet. I want the world to un-

## Chapter 4: SOUNDING TRUMPETS

derstand that evil can rise to the top so smoothly that many will believe that he is God. Please don't be naive, because everything under man's government will come to an end when the Seventh Trumpet sounds. The Sixth Trumpet is the beginning of the end for man's government. It is the most powerful sounding trumpet and the last chance for us to pass our prerequisite courses. Continuing with the Sixth and Seventh Trumpets, we should all be sitting on the edge of our seats as God's final plan is being orchestrated according to His time table.

### Trumpet #6

Revelation 9:13-18:
> And the sixth angel sounded, and I heard a voice from the four horns of the golden altar which is before God, Saying to the sixth angel which had the trumpet, Loose the four angels which are bound in the great river Euphrates. And the four angels were loosed, which were prepared for an hour, and a day, and a month, and a year, for to slay the third part of men. And the number of the army of the horsemen were two hundred thousand thousand: and I heard the number of them. And thus I saw the horses in the vision, and them that sat on them, having breastplates of fire, and of jacinth, and brimstone: and the heads of the horses were as the heads of lions; and out of their mouths issued fire and smoke and brimstone. By these three was the third part of men killed, by the fire, and by the smoke, and by the brimstone, which issued out of their mouths.

The sounding of the Sixth Trumpet tells a fairytale story about the End Times written by Sheralee Snow:

*Once upon a time in a beautiful and perfect place, humans had serenity and peace. But then a crafty devil serpent persuaded the humans to eat from the tree of knowledge of good and evil. Once consumed, evil could never go away. Through generations, evil just kept on controlling the humans. The people continued to pray for a Savior to battle evil. Unfortunately, as evil continued, four dragons were released to work havoc on the world, killing two billion humans. Seeing that this WWIII may never end, a mighty Antichrist arose to contain the four dragons. The people were so happy that the Antichrist arose to gain control over the world again. This leader was so powerful that he seemed to make magical things happen. The people thought he was God. He and his sidekick wanted the people to enjoy all their materialistic things so much that he implemented the Mark of the Beast, a positive trademark, so the people could buy and sell at ease around the world. The people lined up on their jobs to receive the Mark of the Beast. The Antichrist realized some of the people didn't want his trademark, so he ordered death to the traitors. He realized that you can't please everybody, so those that didn't get with his program, would just be eliminated. He sent his soldiers to find and kill the traitors. After all, he was making sure he controlled the people and that they stayed happy and content, and so the traitors must receive death as their reward. The traitors fled to the hills, constantly praying for a Savior*

## Chapter 4: SOUNDING TRUMPETS

*to deal with the Evil One. The Antichrist started to show his evil side even more, and devastation came to God's temple and territory. There arose two end-time Princes who preached about the Kingdom of God and that people had better repent of their sins because the King was coming back. They had power just like the Antichrist, and the Antichrist hated the two Princes. Not only did the Antichrist and his sidekick hate the two Princes, the people hated them also because the two Princes were talking about God's Kingdom and the people thought the Antichrist was God! With the new system in place for buying and selling, things were so simple to manage, and the people were enjoying it. They didn't want to hear about God's Kingdom. After three-and-a-half years, the Antichrist killed the two Princes. The people were happy. Unfortunately, the people never realized they were deceived by the Antichrist; they just went along with the program (Antichrist control). A loud sounding trumpet was heard and a powerful King emerged with his righteous soldiers to combat evil for the last time. The King and his soldiers destroyed the evil ones. The righteous people that died for God were blessed with everlasting life, but for those who took the Mark of the Beast, death was their reward until Judgment Day. The King established a peaceful life for the righteous for one thousand years, a life just like that at the beginning of this story, but without any devilish serpents. The people lived a happy and blessed life and praised God every day.*

## FINAL WAKE-UP CALL

The sounding of the Sixth Trumpet is our final wake-up call; we either pass or fail our prerequisite courses. When the four devilish angels are released, the Sixth Trumpet has sounded. These four devilish angels are from the area around the Euphrates River. They have power the world has never seen before and have been released to work havoc on the world. When the four angels are released they slay a third part of mankind. Two billion people will be destroyed. This will be WWIII, the war of wars. The Bible talks about these four horsemen (angels) that are released to do damage to the world.

In Revelation 6:2-8 we read:
*And I saw, and behold a white horse: and he that sat on him had a bow; and a crown was given unto him: and he went forth conquering, and to conquer. And when he had opened the second seal, I heard the second beast say, Come and see. And there went out another horse that was red: and power was given to him that sat thereon to take peace from the earth, and that they should kill one another: and there was given unto him a great sword. And when he had opened the third seal, I heard the third beast say, Come and see. And I beheld, and lo a black horse; and he that sat on him had a pair of balances in his hand. And I heard a voice in the midst of the four beasts say, A measure of wheat for a penny, and three measures of barley for a penny; and see thou hurt not the oil and the wine. And when he had opened the fourth seal, I heard the voice of the fourth beast say, Come and see. And I*

## Chapter 4: SOUNDING TRUMPETS

*looked, and behold a pale horse: and his name that sat on him was Death, and Hell followed with him. And power was given unto them over the fourth part of the earth, to kill with sword, and with hunger, and with death, and with the beasts of the earth.*

WWIII will be a bloody war with two billion humans dying. During this major destruction the Antichrist and False Prophet will arise. During the Sixth Trumpet we will know the identity of them both. This war will happen because it is God's plan. An army of 200 million soldiers will be involved. China or followers of Islam could field an army of 200 million soldiers today. Many believe that China will be a major player because of their need for oil. The Middle East is the primary place to get oil. The powers of capitalism, communism, and religion could clash in the area along the Euphrates River. I am not here to discuss the identity of the four horsemen. We already know their mission, so regardless of who they are, destruction follows. The world needs to open its eyes to the final end of man's rule. We will either pass or fail the prerequisite courses, so now is not the time to straddle the fence!

The world is in a never-ending, bloody war, and emerging out of the New World Order will be a leader arising to crush the Middle East. A war involving Syria, Iraq, Israel, Iran, Russia, United States of America, Pakistan, China, Korea, Afghanistan and many more triggers this major war of wars—WWIII with the major player (Antichrist) arising as the leader. No country will be exempt from WWIII. The body count will be an enormous tragedy. Sit back and watch with open eyes because WWIII will not come as a surprise to the righteous. During the Sixth Trumpet mankind will finally know the identities of the Antichrist and the False Prophet. During the Sixth Trumpet just keep your eyes open and read, watching all that is happening around the world. Seeing all the events unfold should make us realize that God's plan in Revelation is materializing! God doesn't make any mistakes, but the biggest mistake that mankind has made is in not believing God's Word. Many think that the Sixth Trumpet has already sounded. Now is the time to pass our prerequisite courses before the Seventh Trumpet sounds!

## Trumpet #7

Revelation 11:15-19:
> *And the seventh angel sounded; and there were great voices in heaven, saying, The kingdoms of this world are become the kingdoms of our Lord, and of his Christ; and he shall reign for ever and ever. And the four and twenty elders, which sat before God on their seats, fell upon their faces, and worshipped God, Saying, We give thee thanks, O Lord God Almighty, which art, and wast, and art to come; because thou hast taken to thee thy great power, and hast reigned. And the nations were angry, and thy wrath is come, and the time of the dead, that they should be judged, and that thou shouldest give reward unto thy servants the prophets, and to the saints, and them that fear thy name, small and great; and shouldest destroy them which destroy the earth. And the temple of God was opened in heaven, and there was seen in his temple the ark of his testament: and there were lightnings, and voices, and thunderings, and an earthquake, and great hail.*

## Chapter 4: SOUNDING TRUMPETS

The number seven brings completion—how blessed will the world be when the Seventh Trumpet sounds! The Precious One will return and the battle between good and evil will begin at Armageddon. How long have we been waiting for this battle! It is about time for the Precious One to defeat the Devil and his evil soldiers and supporters.

I am looking forward to this battle between good and evil. I hope that I am living during the End Times. Adam lost the first battle and the Devil won, but the final battle will be won by the Precious One, who achieves victory for God. What a glorious day to be alive and witness good triumph over evil! The Devil couldn't win the final victory. God will know his faithful children, for their names are written in the Book of Life. God gave human beings free will to do what they want. But unfortunately, sin comes with a price, and without repentance and doing God's will, death will be the reward. When the Seventh Trumpet sounds the world has reached its end as the Precious One makes everything right by defeating the Antichrist and all his soldiers. They had become warriors for the Antichrist and their defeat and death will have its terrible sting. The Seventh Trumpet will sound soon!

## *Sounding Trumpet*

No one knows the hour, date, time
For the Precious One's second coming
We know he's coming
As prophecy doesn't lie

Before he returns
Must pass his prerequisite courses
Loving one another
To receive the second Comforter

The sixth trumpet was our test
Pass or fail
Unfortunately with shades of darkness
Many it will be their place of rest

Now I'm telling you the truth
So pay attention now
Don't let the Devil deceive you
Missing a blessed life

Seventh trumpet will sound
Don't think that it won't
So loud and clear, but distinctive
Announcing the King of Kings is here

Pass your courses
I pray today
For those that failed
Now it is too late

Sounding seventh trumpet
God's glory all around
Setting up the Kingdom of God
The Precious One ruling it all

## Chapter 4: SOUNDING TRUMPETS

Please open your eyes to the Sounding Trumpets! It's true that the Precious One will return to battle with the Antichrist. The Seventh Trumpet will announce the battle of Armageddon. Armageddon in Revelation happens during the Seventh Trumpet. Good and evil will battle for the final time. One generation will be a witness to the End Times, and we may be that generation. If we are living during the End Times, we had better pass our prerequisite courses. The righteous have been waiting for the Precious One to return for generations. As the close to this sinful world becomes apparent, what choice will the 50% believers make, a choice that can't be erased and a choice upon which their destiny awaits?

## FINAL WARNING

1. Antichrist and False Prophet—The Mark of the Beast
2. Two End Time Witnesses

God's final action plan includes the ruling of the world by the Antichrist and False Prophet. During the Sixth Trumpet the world will know who the Antichrist and False Prophet are. The One World Order government will be in place and controlled by the Antichrist and his sidekick, the False Prophet. Then God will bless and anoint the two End Time Witnesses to preach his Kingdom. The Antichrist will kill them after three and a half years. Sending the two End Time Witnesses will be God's final act to determine how many of his children will be saved. When the Antichrist kills them, the Seventh Trumpet will sound so loudly that everyone living will look up and witness the return of the Precious One. The Antichrist, False Prophet and the two End

Time witnesses will be discussed in the next two chapters. From the beginning God has had a plan to defeat evil!

## Survival Path

There comes a time
To analyze your mind
A divided path
Only you can find

Twisted relationship
Treated you unkind
Lies, mental breakdown
Survival Path on your mind

Take a stance
Can't straddle the fence
No middle of the road
Your decision must be correct

Same path, self destruction
Hard to let go
Future uncertain
Survival Path only way to go

Devilish behavior
On a sinful life
Must release it all with prayer
If your path is to survive

Take only Godly directions
Honest and true
You know in your heart
Which path is best for you

## Chapter 4: SOUNDING TRUMPETS

Only one direction is rightfully true
That sinful life, leave it behind
Renewed in spirit
Only the true can find

Following the Antichrist
Not the right direction
Eternal hell waits for you
Antichrist path destroyed you

Survival Path
Not easy to achieve
100% Believers
Marching on to victory

Chapter 5

# MARK OF THE BEAST
## *Good and Evil: Devil's ownership*

The final Antichrist will emerge during the sounding of the Sixth Trumpet. He will have a smooth transition to power. With all the economic problems we are incurring every day, his rise to power will be well received, without any consideration of what to expect when he starts to implement his control over mankind. Issues like healthcare, welfare, jobs, terrorism, immigration, education, gun control, and gas prices will be just minor matters when the Antichrist arrives. He'll want power and worship. He will be involved with WWIII, the war that will kill two billion people, making him deadlier than any past antichrist. The Antichrist will be revealed while the four horsemen are causing two billion people to die. The Antichrist will be declared as the Leader/President and the one to stabilize and bring order to the world.

In Revelation 13:1-18 the Bible tells us about the Antichrist:

1. A beast rises up out of the sea, and upon his head is the name of blasphemy.

2. The dragon gives the Antichrist his power, his seat, and great authority.
3. One of his heads was wounded, but his deadly wound was healed and all the world wondered after the beast.
4. They worshipped the dragon and the beast, saying, "Who is like unto the beast? Who is able to make war with him?"
5. There was given unto the beast a mouth speaking great things and blasphemies.
6. The beast was given power for forty and two months.
7. He opened his mouth in blasphemies against God, to blaspheme his name, and his tabernacle, and them that dwell in heaven.
8. It was given to him to make war with the saints and to overcome them.
9. Power was given to him over all kindred, and tongues, and nations.
10. All that dwell upon the earth shall worship him, whose names are not written in the Book of Life of the Lamb slain from the foundation of the world.

If we had any doubts about the ending of man's government, remember that the Antichrist has power for forty and two months, the same time that God's two End Time Witnesses have to preach, teach, and minister about God's Kingdom. Is this timing, three-and-a-half years, a coincidence? At the end of the three-and-a-half years, the Antichrist will kill the two End Time Witnesses. Once the Antichrist completes his mission the Seventh Trumpet sounds and the Precious One is back with a

## Chapter 5: MARK OF THE BEAST

vengeance! Don't be fooled by the order of the events—God's plan is perfect. In the battle between the two, the Precious One and the Antichrist, we will already know our fate.

| GOOD | vs. EVIL |
|---|---|
| The Precious One | The Antichrist |
| Love one another | Devil's Heaven |
| Spiritual mind | Carnal mind |
| Eternal life | Greedy and Materialistic |
| Second Comforter | Failed courses |
| Seal of God | Mark of the Beast |

Seeing the differences between the two while living during the End Times makes us assess our lives. All believers will be put to the test regarding their faith and works, a decision that everyone must make. The Antichrist will be a strong force, as he has a partner who will implement the Mark. Another beast coming up out of the earth will exercise all the power of the first beast before him. This beast, the False Prophet, has to make his appearance because the Antichrist needs his sidekick!

Revelation 13:12-18 tells us:
> *And he exerciseth all the power of the first beast before him, and causeth the earth and them which dwell therein to worship the first beast, whose deadly wound was healed. And he doeth great wonders, so that he maketh fire come down from heaven on the earth in the sight of men, And deceiveth them that dwell on the earth by the means of those miracles which he had power to do in the sight of the beast; saying to them*

*that dwell on the earth, that they should make an image to the beast, which had the wound by a sword, and did live. And he had power to give life unto the image of the beast, that the image of the beast should both speak, and cause that as many as would not worship the image of the beast should be killed. And he causeth all, both small and great, rich and poor, free and bond, to receive a mark in their right hand, or in their foreheads: And that no man might buy or sell, save he that had the mark, or the name of the beast, or the number of his name. Here is wisdom. Let him that hath understanding count the number of the beast: for it is the number of a man; and his number is Six hundred threescore and six.*

## EVIL

The Antichrist and the False Prophet are partners in evil. Things go better with two than one! The Antichrist and False Prophet will control the world government. The False Prophet has power to make people worship the Antichrist and to take his Mark. Don't think the Antichrist's sidekick is not well known in his own right. People follow this False Prophet and have a lot of respect for him. He is known worldwide but he has a devilish side that will emerge, just like his partner the Antichrist. Every believer must understand that the Beast and False Prophet will have great power that has been given to them, but their destruction will be total devastation.

Souls whose names aren't written in the Book of Life will probably worship the Beast. God is letting us know that his children whose names are written in the Book of Life shouldn't

## Chapter 5: MARK OF THE BEAST

worry, because they are protected. Those that worship the Beast and his image, and whosoever receives the mark of his name, will have no rest day or night (Revelation 14:11). God will take care of his flock. If people want to think that the Antichrist is God, let them worship him and take his Mark.

The Mark of the Beast is a negative means to gain control over humans. The Antichrist will brand people like animals letting everyone know that they are his property. Those who are branded will not have everlasting life. The Antichrist is looking for those souls who didn't take his mark. Why? Those souls belong to God, and if those souls die for the cause, their reward is eternal life. Don't be fooled by the Antichrist! 2 Thessalonians 2:3-12 warns us:

> *Let no man deceive you by any means: for that day shall not come, except there come a falling away first, and that man of sin be revealed, the son of perdition; Who opposeth and exalteth himself above all that is called God, or that is worshipped; so that he as God sitteth in the temple of God, shewing himself that he is God. Remember ye not, that, when I was yet with you, I told you these things? And now ye know what withholdeth that he might be revealed in his time. For the mystery of iniquity doth already work: only he who now letteth will let, until he be taken out of the way. And then shall that Wicked be revealed, whom the Lord shall consume with the spirit of his mouth, and shall destroy with the brightness of his coming: Even him, whose coming is after the working of Satan with all power and signs and lying wonders, And with*

*all deceivableness of unrighteousness in them that perish; because they received not the love of the truth, that they might be saved. And for this cause God shall send them strong delusion, that they should believe a lie: That they all might be damned who believed not the truth, but had pleasure in unrighteousness.*

## ANTICHRIST'S CHARACTER

Let's not be fooled about this man, the Antichrist—he does exist, and he is pure evil.

1. Let no man deceive us, because the Antichrist from the beginning will deceive many.
2. A man of sin who has never repented of his sin.
3. The son of perdition, a man who will receive everlasting damnation. Hell will be his reward.
4. He thinks he is God and he wants us to worship him.
5. The Antichrist will be revealed to us in God's time.
6. The Antichrist is a wicked man. The definition of wicked:

    "1. Morally bad; sinful. 2. Marked by playful mischief. 3. Causing harm, trouble, or distress. 4. Obnoxious, as a vile odor." Is this the man we want to worship?

7. The Antichrist will have all power to work signs and lying wonders.
8. With all deceivableness of unrighteousness, all that worship the Antichrist will perish, because they received not the love of the truth.

## Chapter 5: MARK OF THE BEAST

9. The Devil will cause many to be deceived so that they will believe the lie of the Antichrist and never have everlasting life, because they didn't believe God.
10. The Antichrist will be the leader in the One World Government, make no mistake.

The Antichrist is a man who understands his role of deceit. He will understand the economy and what he feels needs to be addressed. He will be all about business and politics. Smart and smooth and so charismatic that many will believe he is God. During the final seven years, he will have three-and-a-half years to bring man under his control, but when he causes the death of the two End Time Witnesses, the Precious One will return to dispose of the Antichrist and his flock of soldiers and the many that took the Mark of the Beast.

### Antichrist

Antichrist emerging
Man of Sin
Sophisticated and handsome
But he just won't win

Draws the crowd
With his lying tongue
Hidden agenda
Fooling the naïve ones

Wants an oath of allegiance
Demanding obedience
Makes his rules
If you play, you lose

WE BELIEVE® The Precious One Is Coming Back

Deceiving many
Believing he's God
As he places his Mark
For all to see

Smooth orator
Persuasive leader
Powerful controller
In a Devil's disguise

Does his miracles
For witnesses to see
He's not God
But do you believe

Shadow of darkness
Rules the world
Wicked Antichrist
Will slowly rot in hell

The Precious One will return to battle
Between good versus evil
Precious One on the winning side
Antichrist, the Beast, will be deceased

Thanks be to God
Praises to the Precious One
Putting an end
To the evil ones

The Precious One
Completed his mission
Has God's blessing
High salute to the King

Chapter 5: MARK OF THE BEAST

## **TRADEMARK**

Understand that God, the Alpha and Omega, is in charge. The Mark of the Beast makes perfect sense, for God will know his chosen children, the ones that refused to be branded like animals. The Mark of the Beast is a test of our faith. Satan has been running loose and we have been blinded by his crafty ways, kept in the dark. We have become a materialistic society and if people can't pay for the material things they love (house, cars, etc.) without the mark, they just won't know how to survive. Even knowing the truth about the Mark of the Beast, most can't wait to receive it! The Bible is clear on what happens to those who take the mark. Revelation 14:9-11 warns:

> *And the third angel followed them, saying with a loud voice, If any man worship the beast and his image, and receive his mark in his forehead, or in his hand, The same shall drink of the wine of the wrath of God, which is poured out without mixture into the cup of his indignation; and he shall be tormented with fire and brimstone in the presence of the holy angels, and in the presence of the Lamb: And the smoke of their torment ascendeth up for ever and ever: and they have no rest day nor night, who worship the beast and his image, and whosoever receiveth the mark of his name.*

If we are living during the implementation of the Mark of the Beast, not taking it will be a great gift to God. What a show of unconditional love and faith to stand up and say no to the Mark of the Beast! Satan has ruled this earth and we are blinded by his patterns of deceit to lead us away from the truth. God knows the ending to His story:

> *And the beast was taken, and with him the false prophet that wrought miracles before him, with which he deceived them that had received the mark of the beast, and them that worshipped his image. These both were cast alive into a lake of fire burning with brimstone.* (Revelation 19:20)

Some have been marked by the beast already—it's just not a physical mark. We have forgotten the Lord's commandments and statutes. We have learned how to justify the wrongs that we have inflicted on others. Not only have people not repented from their sins, they have justified their choices.

## Mark of The Beast

Living in luxury
Fancy cars, limousines
Beautiful mansions
Castles, can't you see
Fast yachts, powerful jets
Must keep up with
Modern technology you bet

Living the lie
Money flowing
Constantly growing
Morocco, France, Canada
Italy, Barbados, Brazil

## Chapter 5: MARK OF THE BEAST

You name the place
No holding you back
High self-esteem
You don't lack

Living in style
Clothes galore
Matching hats and shoes
Tapered cut and fitting tight
Gucci, Coach, Ralph Lauren
Sean John, Louis Vuitton, to name a few
Looking sharp
In leather too

Living on the hill
No site too high
Consistently climbing
Leaving obstacles with no end
Decisive backstabbing path
Only you can find
Consistently raping
What you left behind

Living for power
Controlling freak
Greed, lust,
Can't get enough
Absolute control
Lies to behold
Your games and rules
You play, can't lose

Living for the mark
Keep what you got
Buy, sell, status quo
That's the only way to go
Easy choice, physical mark
Beastie system in the dark
Think you have control
Devil has your mind, body and soul

Living for Satan
Satan gotcha now
Materialistic you
Boy, did you lose
Lost your soul
Can't undo
The mark so apparent
Unfortunately God
Has no room for you

## THE DECISION

Unfortunately, we can't straddle the fence when the mark is offered to us. It has always been easier to take a neutral position, neither for nor against, but with the mark that just isn't possible. We must make a choice—a choice that will affect our lives forever. We have been surrounded by the beast every day. The worldly "beastie system" has been in place ever since Satan has been free to roam this earth. It's amazing how far we have moved, from first base to third base, right field to left field, never trying for the middle in order to receive the truth. Man has lusted after the flesh.

## Chapter 5: MARK OF THE BEAST

*For the love of money is the root of all evil: which while some coveted after, they have erred from the faith, and pierced themselves through with many sorrows. But thou, O man of God, flee these things; and follow after righteousness, godliness, faith, love, patience, meekness. Fight the good fight of faith, lay hold on eternal life, whereunto thou art also called, and hast professed a good profession before many witnesses.* (1 Timothy 6:10-12)

We have become a materialistic world, and the choice of taking the Mark of the Beast will test our faith. The Antichrist is an evil man who will gain absolute power and will try to brand us like cattle. Those who resist and die for their faith will receive the reward of everlasting life!

Currently we do not know who the Antichrist is, but God left us a blueprint to follow so that during the Sixth Trumpet we will find out who the Antichrist and False Prophet are. As soon as the End Time Witnesses are killed by the Antichrist the Seventh Trumpet will sound. Daniel 9:24 tells us, *"Seventy weeks are determined upon thy people and upon thy holy city, to finish the transgression, and to make an end of sins, and to make reconciliation for iniquity, and to bring in everlasting righteousness, and to seal up the vision and prophecy, and to anoint the most Holy."* Ken Raggio, in his article, "Daniel's Seventy Weeks Prophecies," says, "A 'week of years' in prophecy is seven years." This article lays out a virtual calendar of six events for the last days. Irvin Baxter, in *Endtime Magazine*, Nov/Dec 2008 cover story, "Prophetic Implications of Obama's Revolution," discusses nine specific prophecies in the Bible that will occur within the final seven years prior to the Battle of Armageddon. Regardless of which events I list, we are looking at *the most important seven years* in all the history of the world heretofore! I have nine events that will happen during the seven year plan, similar to both Ken Raggio and Irvin Baxter.

## SEVEN YEAR PLAN

1. The Seven Year plan starts when the principal parties sign the Covenant of Peace. The Antichrist and the False Prophet, with approval from the international community, will give their support to Israel's right to exist in the land promised by God to Abraham. This is usually referred to as the "Confirmation of the Covenant."

2. World War III will begin in the area around the Euphrates River. This war will kill over two billion people—the war of wars, with huge slaughter in Judea.

3. The Jewish Temple will be built on the Temple Mount in Jerusalem under the direction of the Antichrist. He will believe that he is God and convince many souls to believe it, too.

4. The World Government will dominate the world for three-and-a-half-years.

5. Desolation in the temple will occur at the middle of the Seven Year plan. The Antichrist will commit the Abomination of Desolation in the Temple.

6. The Antichrist has only 3½ years left to implement his government. He implements the Mark of the Beast, Revelation 13:16-17:

   *And he caused all, both small and great, rich and poor, free and bond, to receive a mark in their right hand, or in their foreheads: And that no man might buy or sell, save he that*

## Chapter 5: MARK OF THE BEAST

had the mark, or the name of the beast, or the number of his name.

7. During these three-and-a-half years God's two End Time Witnesses will prophesy. Revelation 11:3-6:

   *And I will give power unto my two witnesses, and they shall prophesy a thousand two hundreds and threescore days, clothed in sackcloth. These are the two olive trees, and the two candlesticks standing before the God of the earth. And if any man will hurt them, fire proceedeth out of their mouth, and devoureth their enemies: and if any man will hurt them, he must in this manner be killed. These have the power to shut heaven, that it rain not in the days of their prophecy: and have power over waters to turn them to blood, and to smite the earth with all plagues, as often as they will.*

8. The Antichrist after three-and-a-half years will kill the two End Time Witnesses. Revelation 11:7-13:

   *And when they shall have finished their testimony, the beast that ascendeth out of the bottomless pit shall make war against them, and shall overcome them, and kill them. And their dead bodies shall lie in the street of the great city, which spiritually is called Sodom and Egypt, where also our Lord was crucified. And they of the people and kindreds and tongues and nations shall see their dead bodies three days and an half, and shall not suffer their dead bodies to be put in graves. And they that dwell upon the earth shall rejoice over them, and make merry, and shall send gifts one to another; because these two prophets tormented them that dwelt on the earth. And after three days and an half the Spirit of life from God entered into them, and they stood upon their feet; and great fear fell upon them which saw them. And they heard a great voice from heaven saying unto them, Come up hither. And they ascended up to heaven in a cloud; and their enemies beheld them. And the same hour was there a great earthquake, and the tenth part of the city fell, and in the earthquake were slain of men seven thousand: and the remnant were affrighted, and gave glory to the God of heaven.*

9. The Seventh Trumpet sounds; the Precious One will return with all saints; the Battle of Armageddon will be fought and won by the Precious One.

We will know who the Antichrist and False Prophet are with the Confirmation of the Covenant. The Third Temple will be built because the Antichrist wants to show the world that he is God. He wants to possess God's holy territory. If he wants people to believe that he is God, he must do it in God's territory. In the Bible we are told that God's holy area was around Mount Moriah. God has always called his people to this holy mountain. Abraham was called to this mountain top. The Precious One spoke to the people on Mount Moriah. Moses delivered the Ten Commandments from the mountaintop and David built an altar there. Understand that the temple must be built, and when we witness the Confirmation of the Covenant it will be built! The Third Temple will be built as part of the execution of God's plan for the end of evil. The Seven Year Plan will begin. The Antichrist will mark his people; the masses will take the mark.

Chapter 5: MARK OF THE BEAST

## CHOICES

A decision must be made during the time of the Antichrist. His power will be huge and totally controlling. I really don't think we understand what all of this means. I believe we need a wake-up call! Let's back up and reread Revelation 13:16-17:

> *And he causeth all, both small and great, rich and poor, free and bond, to receive a mark in their right hand, or in their foreheads: And that no man might buy or sell, save he that had the mark, or the name of the beast, or the number of his name.*

Do you think we will be exempted? That description is for all. So what does it mean? I'm going to make it very simple for us to understand the Mark of the Beast—language that we can understand! Let's start with the American Dream: a nice brick two-story house, with basement, white picket fence, and two cars. First, how are we to pay the mortgage and car note without the mark? Did we say we won't take the mark? Let's go inside the house: nice stainless steel appliances (Sub Zero), love your walnut hardwood floors, did I see a "sleep number" bed?, your art work is to die for! But how do we pay when we can't use our credit cards? Did we say we won't take the mark? Can I look into your closet? So many shoes and clothes, girl, you have a rainbow of colors for every situation. How do we pay for all this? We didn't take the mark? We've got Wi-Fi and a nice computer. How do we pay for the electricity bill? We didn't take the mark? Love to eat out? How do we pay the bill? I believe we need the Mark of the Beast!

Do we understand now? Everything that we do involves

buying and selling and, without the Mark, we cannot pay for anything. I can foresee many people who can't wait to receive it, lining up for the Mark of the Beast on their job. It will not be a hard choice for many, but I hope people will remember what the Mark means for their destiny. I know we all have brothers and sisters incarcerated and they can't take the Mark. A hard decision must be made by all, but if we believe in the Word, the choice is easy. The process may be hard, but the reward is eternal life! Revelation 20:4 gives us the answer:

> *And I saw thrones, and they sat upon them, and judgment was given unto them: and I saw the souls of them that were beheaded for the witness of Jesus, and for the word of God, and which had not worshipped the beast, neither his image, neither had received his mark upon their foreheads, or in their hands; and they lived and reigned with Christ a thousand years.*

Did we read it? It's a simple choice for survival—say no to the Mark! Those living during the time of the Antichrist who take the Mark will not have everlasting life. It's our decision, not God's. Is our faith stronger than our materialistic desires? How many people do we know who will take the Mark of the Beast? I hope and pray that if we are living during the End Times we will know that we cannot take it. Our lives will end if we take that Mark.

I can see how easily the Mark of the Beast could be implemented. Just imagine working on our jobs when the human resource manager tells us they are doing away with paperwork and implementing a new, convenient system that will make our lives so simple! No more problems with fraud on our accounts, a "beastie simple system" to buy and sell. I can see everyone lining up for the new system and not even being aware of what they are taking. That's why my mission is to make it clear and easy for God's children to understand. The Mark of the Beast will take place and we must flee from taking it.

Now, we must realize that the Precious One's return is not about saving us. The Precious One has a mission to end all the evil that has been allowed to run rampant. He's coming back to defeat evil and establish God's Kingdom. The Precious One will not have time to tell us, "Now that you see me do you believe?" It will be too late for us to repent. Nothing on this earth could ever make me take the Mark of the Beast, because I believe. Test your faith!

## Test Of Faith

A simple test of faith
No studying is required
No caffeine to keep you up
 Just a simple answer
As your future unfolds

Thought you studied hard
Brilliant in your class
Multiple choices, true or false
Not allowed – Pass or Fail
Wrong answer- May you rest in hell

## WE BELIEVE  The Precious One Is Coming Back

Thought you had the answer
Simple you thought
Oh what a misunderstanding
Believing in the Antichrist
From the start

Can't dot the i's or
Cross the t's
Can't look over your shoulder
Cheating
Won't set you free

No second chance
On test of faith
Just one answer is allowed
Can't place on hold
While you decide

Wondering how to answer
Not sure of the results
Scared, frightened, can't decide
What a major decision
Heavy on your mind

Common sense might help
Past actions too quick to judge
No one in your corner
Can't look for an answer
From heaven above

Don't take the test
Automatically fail
No future plans
No hope in sight
On everlasting life

## Chapter 5: MARK OF THE BEAST

God must test our faith
At the End of Time,
But understand
The Precious One can't undo
The Mark of the Beast that's on you

God is smiling, The Precious One
Defeated the beast
Victory to the souls
That knew exactly
Which way to go

## Chapter 6

# END TIME WITNESSES
## *Good and Evil: final exam*

This chapter about the two End Time Witnesses is a must read. It is so symbolic, and through it God reveals the truth to all. If those living during the End Times can't see the truth of how evil the world is and understand that we control our own destiny, then shame on us! The final blueprint plan plays out like a fairytale story written by Sheralee Snow:

> Once upon a time an evil Devil ruled the world. The Devil would do miracles so that the people would think he was God. During his reign, four destructive dragons were released to slay one-third part of mankind through whatever means possible. The Devil contained the four dragons and they became his army of soldiers.
>
> The Devil with his mighty army started to deceive the people by branding them with his mark. They couldn't buy or sell without his mark. Most of the people were completely blind, taking the Devil's trademark without

*a second look to evaluate the pros and cons, because they thought he was God.*

*The people who didn't take the mark fled to the hills and mountains. The Devil issued an order: "Death to the traitors." The Devil sent his army to kill the traitors. The believers knew they couldn't take the Devil's mark, because they believed the King would come and rescue them from the evil Devil. Their prayers were being answered, and there arose two princes that were teaching and preaching about the King who was coming to establish God's Kingdom. They were telling the good news about the beautiful Kingdom of God and how the Devil was deceiving the people.*

*The people hated the two princes and wished they were dead. The Devil knew he couldn't harm the two princes for three-and-a-half years. The Devil was upset because that would give the people who didn't take the Devil's mark time to pass their prerequisite courses. With the constant preaching from the two princes, the Devil destroyed the Third Temple on God's holy land. The people were still in the dark and enjoying the new beastie system. The two princes continued spreading the good news, telling the people to repent and receive the second Comforter of life, the righteous blood of the King.*

*Unfortunately, the people didn't believe them, and when the Devil killed them, the people were happy.*

Chapter 6: END TIME WITNESSES

*Upon their death, God raised his two princes and brought them home. An earthquake shook the foundation, but it was too late for the 50% believers to enter the Golden Gates of Paradise. They never understood what Devil's Heaven was all about and they never passed their prerequisite courses. The Devil made sure the people became his property by taking his trademark, the Mark of the Beast, and they would therefore never receive eternal life.*

*The Seventh Trumpet sounded and the King of Kings appeared with all the blessed saints. It was a beautiful and perfect gathering as the King of Kings dealt with the evil one and his posse and established God's Kingdom. God's people lived and enjoyed a peaceful and beautiful paradise with the King.*

## PROPHECY

Two people are blessed and anointed by God to prophesy about the Kingdom of God and the true Church of God. They have only three-and-a-half years to complete their mission, and then they are killed by the Antichrist, and then the Precious One returns. That's the blueprint plan finale ending with the two End Time Witnesses' death at the sounding of the Seventh Trumpet and the glory of the Precious One's return.

This chapter will be difficult for many, because for centuries many churches have drifted away from the true Church of God. Understand that God knows our heart and the doctrines that we have followed, but the truth will hurt many and many will not believe the End Time Witnesses. As believers, we know that Acts 2:38 states: *"Then Peter said unto them, Repent, and be baptized every one of you in the name of Jesus Christ for the remission of sins, and ye shall receive the gift of the Holy Ghost."* It should be apparent that we must pass our prerequisite courses to receive the second Comforter rewarded by God. We need to receive this special gift.

As we read this chapter about the End Time Witnesses, we will know exactly what and why we have been blindly led to believe in the doctrines of so many churches. The truth must be told by the End Time Witnesses to try to save others from destruction by the Antichrist. Believers already know that many things will change when we learn about the true Church of God. The churches with their false leaders will be dealt with by the Precious One.

After three-and-a-half years, the Antichrist is the only one who can give permission to kill God's two End Time Witnesses. God has orchestrated everything from the beginning to the end. As you read this chapter, please have an open mind and heart to receive God's truth as it will be taught by his two End Time Witnesses, who are described in the King James Version of the Bible, Revelation 11:3-13:

1. God gives them power and they have three-and-a-half years to complete their mission. These two people have been anointed by God and are given the free will to preach by any means. They have power to shut down heaven so that it doesn't rain during their prophecy. They even have power over water to turn it to blood. When they use their powers, will people believe they were sent by God?

## Chapter 6: END TIME WITNESSES

2. The two End Time witnesses are special people. They are described as two olive trees and the two candlesticks standing before the God of the earth. They have the unique job of telling the truth about God's Kingdom and Church. They are grounded in the truth of God.

3. Nobody had better try to hurt these two End Time Witnesses, for they have the power to devour their enemies! If any man hurts them, he must in this manner be killed. The Antichrist is the only one able to kill them, and he will be dealt with by the Precious One.

4. Once dead, their bodies will be exposed before all as they lay in the street. It will be on all TV networks, and many will be happy that the two witnesses, who caused so many problems, are dead. Their bodies will lie in the street for three-and-a-half days.

5. Most people that dwell upon the earth will rejoice over their dead bodies and will be happy, sending gifts to each other.

6. After three-and-a-half days, the Spirit of life from God will enter the two witnesses and they will stand upon their feet. Great fear will fall upon those who saw them.

7. They will ascend up to heaven in a cloud.

8. During the same hour there will be a great earthquake killing seven thousand people.

9. The Seventh Trumpet will sound, announcing the return of the Precious One.

These two End Time Witnesses have been predetermined by God. When it is time for their mission God will make it known to them. If we are living while they prophesy, we will hear and see how people won't be able to stand them. They won't believe the witnesses are telling the truth about God's Kingdom and Church. The truth will be hard to hear, but as long as we continue obeying God and if we pass the Precious One's commandment and have repented for our sins, the truth will set us free. The witnesses' ministry must get to the core of God's Church, and that's why the Antichrist hates these two witnesses. He knows they are from God and that they are telling the truth about him, the Devil's messiah.

The Antichrist has deceived so many that the people now believe he is God. The Antichrist will kill these two opponents, but not until three-and-a-half years. The problem for many during the witnesses' three-and-a-half years is that many have taken the Mark of the Beast. They have believed the lie of the Antichrist and think the two witnesses must be lying. It is easy to be deceived, but even when the inner ear tells them that these two witnesses might be telling the truth, they won't be able to erase the Mark of the Beast. The two End Time Witnesses are the last step before the Precious One returns, as they continue spreading the Good News. We had better pass our prerequisite courses! The two End Time Witnesses are blessed. They will minister to the world about God's Kingdom and God's Church, exposing false leaders. The lies from the false churches will be exposed.

## *End Time Witnesses*

Two End Time Witnesses
Blessed and anointed by God
Given all power
Preaching and ministering to all

## Chapter 6: END TIME WITNESSES

Have 3½ years
To complete their mission
Don't get in their way or
Darkness is your prison

Witnesses know the outcome
Blessed are they
Their hearts pure and true
Hoping 50% believers have repented too

Power to change things
Don't hurt them at all
Antichrist hates them
Bottomless pit he will fall

Turning water to blood
Plagues to smite the earth
Non-Believers are you
Believing their works

Can't change their future
Antichrist will destroy
But praise be to God
Witnesses completed their mission

As their dead bodies
Lie in the street
Joy and merry
Praising the beast

After 3½ days
Their souls will rise
As God sweeps them up
To heaven up high

> 7th trumpet sounds
> Look high to the sky
> The Precious One has returned
> Armageddon, the Bible didn't lie
>
> God's blessed Believers
> They knew the truth
> The Precious One adorned in white
> Victory, the battle finished tonight

## THE TRUTH

The End Time Witnesses have humbled themselves and they are all about doing the will of God. They must have ammunition to back up their preaching. Now the world will see that they can fight back, putting plagues on the land and destroying those who want to kill them. The truth will blind many into hating these two anointed people. What truths can they say that will cause many to dislike them? I couldn't imagine what the End Time Witnesses would say to make so many people hate them.

Then I read a book by Ronald Weinland, *2008: God's Final Witness*. This book was very interesting, and even though some of his predictions didn't materialize as written, he made a statement that needs to be addressed. In his first chapter, "God's Two Witnesses," under the topic *Next Step*, he writes:

> *It is now with boldness, confidence and great clarity that I give to you what God has given me. I am to announce, through God's direct revelation, that I am one of those two witnesses. The other witness will be revealed to the world during the time of the great*

## Chapter 6: END TIME WITNESSES

> *tribulation—within the final three-and-one-half years of man's era. During that period of time, we will, together, completely fulfill all that God has given us to witness to this whole earth. Then, at the end, we will die in the streets of Jerusalem; and finally, exactly three-and-one-half days later, we will be resurrected (Revelation 11). The world will see this resurrection via television. At this same time Jesus Christ will appear in the heavens above the earth as He is returning to take the reigns of man's government on earth.*

I believe that when it is time for God's two End Time Witnesses to emerge, they will be anointed and ready to preach about God's Kingdom and God's true Church. I am not judging Ronald Weinland—if he has been anointed by God to be an End Time Witness, what a glorious blessing! I was excited to hear what he would be preaching about during the End Times. Ronald Weinland continues in Chapter 2, "The Deception In Man":

> *One of the harshest realities people can face is to learn that they have been lied to about their religious beliefs—that they have been deceived. This is one of the most difficult barriers in life to break. People instinctively defend their beliefs because they are foundational to their entire outlook on life—the core of their decision-making process in all matters of life.*

The author then discusses the worst offenders. As I read about them I could see why the masses of people will hate the two witnesses.

Weinland continues Chapter 2:

> *Religion is the greatest culprit of all when it comes to lying and deceit. You need to know why! It is for this very reason that this earth is about to suffer more than it has at any other time in history. Religion has had a devastating impact on people in all nations of the world. The clash of lying religions is about to erupt on a worldwide scale that will affect every person on earth.*

He then continues to talk about false teaching, covering topics like:

- Good Friday/Easter—not three days and three nights (Do the math!)
- Sunday worship
- Trinity
- Christmas and Easter—pagan worship
- Communion, Lent

Ronald Weinland's book breaks down the above topics for understanding and clarity, showing why they are false doctrines. In Chapter 7, "The Mystery of God Revealed," he discusses Passover:

> *In 325 A.D., the Catholic Church convened the Council of Nicea. I will simply cover the highlights of this momentous event.*
>
> *The Passover was in controversy and the Catholic Church wanted to be rid of it, since it wanted to be*

## Chapter 6: END TIME WITNESSES

*fully separate from all ties that associated it with the true Church of God, which faithfully observed the yearly Passover. It also wanted to distance itself from Judaism. The annual observance of Passover was replaced with the observance of Easter, which itself was rife with pagan practices (eggs, rabbits, fertility, hot cross buns, sunrise worship of the sun god, the resurrection of Tammuz, and the queen of heaven – Ishtar and Ashtoreth).*

*God did not establish a holy observance for the resurrection of Jesus Christ, but only for his death in the observance of the yearly Passover. The Catholic Church even perverted the Passover observance by instituting weekly Communion. The taking of a piece of unleavened bread and the drinking of a small amount of wine is a yearly observance God commanded His Church, called Passover, which represents the religious significance of Christ's broken body and the blood that He poured out for our sins.*

*By substituting Easter for Passover, the Catholic Church was also attempting to give credibility to Sunday worship rather than the seventh-day Sabbath. By observing Easter and saying that Jesus Christ was resurrected at sunrise on a Sunday morning, it could then say Christ should be worshipped on Sundays. But as it has been stated, Jesus Christ had already risen before Sunday even began. He was resurrected just prior to sundown on the seventh day, before the first day of the week began. God gave man the method of how to count a day, counting from the moment of sundown of one day to the moment of sundown of the*

> next. As an example, throughout the Bible the weekly seventh-day Sabbath was always observed from sundown on the sixth day (Friday) to sundown on the seventh day (Saturday). The early Greeks and Romans used the method of counting a day from midnight to midnight.
>
> Not only did the Council of Nicea seek to destroy the true identity of Jesus Christ by instituting Easter, it also sought to destroy knowledge of the true identity of the Eternal God by instituting the perverted, sick and damnable doctrine of the Trinity. These two doctrines have been Satan's greatest and most fruitful attempts to deceive mankind into greater ignorance of who Jesus Christ and God the father are. The identity and revelation of who the true Jesus Christ is was covered in "The Prophesied End Time."

Ronald Weinland continues from his book, *2008: God's Final Witness*, in Chapter 2, "The Deception In Man":

> The more you learn about the differences in doctrines within Christianity, as well as their origins, the more lies and deception you will discover. Do yourself a favor and check an encyclopedia for words like Christmas, Easter, Trinity, and Sabbath and see what you learn. You will find that some doctrines of traditional Christianity have much of their origin in paganism. These things don't seem to bother people, but it should! If something is not fully of God, then it is not of God, and it is not true!

## Chapter 6: END TIME WITNESSES

His book is very interesting, and he goes on to comment in Chapter 7, "The Mystery of God Revealed":

> *Any religious groups holding to any of these false doctrines are themselves false! They received these false doctrines from the Catholic Church. Easter is nowhere mentioned in the Bible. The Mass of Christ (Christmas) is nowhere mentioned in scripture. The Trinity is not mentioned in the Bible anywhere, and neither are any of these other false doctrines I have mentioned. They are fables of the Catholic Church and God condemns them all. God is getting ready to destroy every false religion and everyone who insists on holding onto them. If you have any desire to live into the new world that is coming, then you must repent of these false doctrines you have been embracing.*

In addition, Weinland states in Chapter 2:

> *All the "Christian" churches that embrace Sunday worship, Easter and Christmas observance, and the Trinity doctrine received these doctrines through the Catholic Church; yet all these churches believe that many doctrines, which the Catholic Church embraces to be spiritually true, are false.*

If the two End Time Witnesses are preaching about the Church of God and Ron Weinland is accurate in what he says about the topics above, then it is clear why the two End Time Witnesses are hated by masses of people. Most people believe their religion is telling the truth, but unfortunately as I stated at the beginning of this book, most religions fall short of the true Church of God. The hardest thing that most must face is that the Devil had a big part in changing God's doctrines to false doctrines. The Devil was crafty at the beginning in the Garden of Eden and he has never stopped deceiving man by means of religion. Don't get mad at the two witnesses; get glad, no matter who the two End Time Witnesses turn out to be. They will be telling the truth, and those who don't believe are just lost souls.

## Lost Souls

Lost souls
There will be many
Not repenting from sin
It will cost them plenty

Lost souls
That didn't believe
Took the Mark
From the beast that deceived

Lost souls
No self-discipline
Stayed in Devil's Heaven
Till the bitter end

Lost souls
They had a choice
Picking Satan
Ended their life

Lost souls
Thought they were right
But guided by the devil
Darkness all night

Lost souls
It's so sad
50% believers
Lacked self-control

Lost souls
Didn't understand
Straddling the fence
Cost them their soul

## MY BELIEFS

I was baptized in my family church, Kyles Temple A.M.E. Zion, in Sacramento, California, and I have since joined a Baptist Church in Riverdale, Georgia. I have always felt that all churches fall short of the true Church of God, but that hasn't stopped me from joining a church of Bible believers. I never could understand how the period from Good Friday to early sunrise on Sunday could be the interval before the resurrection of the Precious One, because it doesn't add up to three days and three nights. I never did understand why we worship on Sunday rather than the Sabbath, as God instructed, until I studied and learned how manmade religion changed the day. Of course, I did realize that Christmas, Easter, and Halloween were not mentioned in the Bible, yet I participated in all those holidays growing up. Some doctrines just didn't seem right, but it never stopped me from gaining more knowledge and feeding my soul concerning God and the Precious One.

The two End Time Witnesses will tell the truth about God's Church and Kingdom. What a revelation to hear the truth, and how many false teachings will be exposed! The two End Time Witnesses are anointed by God and God doesn't lie. Their preaching will fall on the deaf ears of the nonbelievers. God is waking up his children for the last time. The Antichrist will be controlling the world and deceiving everyone into thinking he is God. The Antichrist has always wanted what God has. Unfortunately, he will end in destruction along with the False Prophet and their followers. The End Time Witnesses are revealing the meaning of God's prophecies and that God will bring all earthly government to an end.

I pray that all members of a church will open their ears to the truth and receive the Good News. Nearly everyone has been blinded to God's true Church. We need to read the history of some of the most powerful churches and where their roots lie. The believers know that by repenting of our sins, receiving the Precious One's Comforter, and continuing to have unshakable faith and works, we will be blessed. The believers know that many false prophets have misguided their flock and we will learn about the true Church of God and embrace it. The End Time Witnesses are coming after the false leaders who have deceived people about God's Church. These leaders are the ones who have fed the masses with lies. The Precious One is coming back, and he will deal with the false churches ruled by false prophets, antichrists, and false leaders. We must continue doing what the Precious One has said and strive to pass our prerequisite courses, so that God will bless us to receive the second Comforter and enjoy everlasting life!

## THE END

The two End Time Witnesses will be killed by the Antichrist and then the Seventh Trumpet will sound. Revelation 14:1-5 tells us what happens then:

> *And I looked, and, lo, a Lamb stood on the mount Sion, and with him an hundred forty and four thousand, having his Father's name written in their foreheads. And I heard a voice from heaven, as the voice of many waters, and as the voice of a great thunder: and I heard the voice of harpers harping with their harps: And they sung as it were a new song before the throne, and before the four beasts, and the elders: and no man could learn that song but the hundred and forty and four thousand, which were redeemed from the earth. These are they which were not defiled with women; for they are virgins. These are they which follow the Lamb whithersoever he goeth. These were redeemed from among men, being the firstfruits unto God and to the Lamb. And in their mouth was found no guile: for they are without fault before the throne of God.*

The 144,000 servants have the seal of God in their foreheads. The 144,000 servants are from the tribes of the children of Israel (Jacob), as follows: (Ten tribes from Israel's sons and two tribes from Joseph's sons, Israel's grandsons. Source: www.ancienthistory.about.com.)

- Tribe of Judah         12,000 servants sealed
- Tribe of Reuben        12,000 servants sealed
- Tribe of Gad           12,000 servants sealed
- Tribe of Asher         12,000 servants sealed
- Tribe of Naphtali      12,000 servants sealed
- Tribe of Manasseh*     12,000 servants sealed
- Tribe of Simeon        12,000 servants sealed
- Tribe of Issachar      12,000 servants sealed
- Tribe of Zebulun       12,000 servants sealed
- Tribe of Benjamin      12,000 servants sealed
- Tribe of Dan           12,000 servants sealed
- Tribe of Ephraim*      12,000 servants sealed

(*Manasseh and Ephraim, Jacob's grandsons) Two brothers were scolded by Israel for taking revenge for their sister, Dinah, who was raped. As punishment Levi was not assigned a territory.

These 144,000 servants were redeemed from the earth. They are the ones that return to earth with the Precious One. In addition, God remembers his faithful souls that were *"beheaded for the witness of Jesus, and for the word of God, and which had not worshipped the beast, neither his image, neither had received his mark upon their foreheads, or in their hands; and they lived and reigned with Christ a thousand years. But the rest of the dead lived not again until the thousand years were finished. This is the first resurrection"* (Revelation 20:4-5).

## Chapter 6: END TIME WITNESSES

Blessed and holy are the people who have a part in the first resurrection! These are the people that believed in God and the Precious One. They are the true 100% believers that repented of their sins and by their faith and works are resurrected from human beings to spiritual beings. They reign with the Precious One and the 144,000 servants for a thousand years. After the thousand years the dead will have their Judgment Day:

> *And I saw the dead, small and great, stand before God; and the books were opened: and another book was opened, which is the book of life: and the dead were judged out of those things which were written in the books, according to their works. And the sea gave up the dead which were in it; and death and hell delivered up the dead which were in them: and they were judged every man according to their works. And death and hell were cast into the lake of fire. This is the second death. And whosoever was not found written in the book of life was cast into the lake of fire.* (Revelation 20:12–15)

Judgment Day is real, and if our names are not written in the Book of Life we didn't make it to the touchdown zone! The second death will have its sting and sizzle.

### Touchdown Zone

Alpha and Omega
Beginning and end
Time will run out
Which zone will you finish in

## WE BELIEVE® The Precious One Is Coming Back

No breaking God's promise
10, 20, 30, 40 even 50 yards won't do
Touchdown zone
Must score can't lose

Taking God's direction
Honest and true
Knowing in your heart
Which zone is best for you

That sinful life
Must be left behind
Renewed in spirit
Only the true can find

Touchdown zone
Not easy to achieve
But keep on running
Obstacles will cease to be

Everyone must decide
Individual choice
Faith and works
Always went side by side

Time is running out
Back stepping not allowed
Face to face situation
Can't fade into the crowd

End of time coming soon
Judgment Day can't escape
Touchdown zone must be in
Or lake of fire is the end

Chapter 6: END TIME WITNESSES

## PASS OR FAIL

The End Time Witnesses will preach God's truths. They will have a tough job to do, especially when the world is ruled by a One World Government and one ruler. The chances are that many will take the Mark of the Beast for survival, but it will be just like Eve listening to the serpent. The Antichrist's and the serpent's messages are full of lies, but unfortunately, the Antichrist will win with the Mark of the Beast. Don't be scared to say no to the mark, just remember that death has no sting if we believe. Knowing the truth about God's love for his children and the blessing of having eternal life should make the choice easier. Listen to what the End Time Witnesses are saying, and don't be in a hurry to sign up for the Mark of the Beast.

The world is getting worse by the day. In the United States of America we see the horrible mess some are making regarding healthcare for all. God must be very disappointed with many who are fighting this issue, because the government is doing the right thing for the people. God cares about the people, but unfortunately many don't believe in a democracy that helps all. There will be many more issues and problems for the President of the United States to deal with, especially since he is dealing with many members of the Superior Devil Shield Club. It's no wonder that the Devil is working overtime to destroy many issues that benefit the American people. Understand the United States of America will have plenty of interior battles that will push it into WWIII. We all know what the Devil will try to destroy: government, IRS, Social Security, the Affordable Care Act, immigration, minimum wage, voter rights and others. Anything that is good for Americans under the leadership of President Barack Obama, the devils will try to destroy. Do you see any, "Love One Another"?

We need to pass our prerequisite courses and receive the Precious One's Comforter before the sounding of the Seventh Trumpet. It's the final test to see where our faith, works, mind and heart are. If we don't pass the prerequisite courses we will never receive the second Comforter. The Precious One doesn't hand out his Comforter to anyone who doesn't love others and God will not reward us with the second Comforter at all. It will be a very hard course to pass during the End Times, because people are set in their ways, enjoying Devil's Heaven.

Chapter 7

# WE BELIEVE
## *Good and Evil: Battle of Armageddon*

The End Times marks the ending of man's government. It has been long overdue—God's children have suffered through blood, sweat, and tears for generations. We have endured the darkness of man—killers, murderers, rapists, and pure evil against those who are different or have the wrong pedigree. We have endured the silent killers: poverty, hunger, starvation, poor health, diseases and homelessness. It has affected all races, and the righteous have prayed on bloody knees for centuries.

God has answered all the prayers and dried all the tears, signaling that the light is coming and will never burn out. God never intended his children to live like this. God knows the pain and hardship we have faced and endured. From the beginning God's plan has been in place to bring an end to man's government. Evil had to be stopped once and for all. Evil and sin cannot reign in God's Kingdom. 1 John 3:8 says, *"He that committeth sin is of the devil; for the devil sinneth from the beginning. For this purpose the Son of God was manifested, that he might destroy the works of the devil."*

God is bringing an end to the evil ones and destroying the works of the Devil. God had a perfect relationship with Adam and Eve until the Devil convinced Eve to eat from the tree of knowledge of good and evil. The Devil's words to Eve have caused humans to die for their disobedience to God. The Devil's words in Genesis 3:4, *"Ye shall not surely die,"* have been our downfall since the beginning of man. Once Adam had sinned, all of his fruits would be the works of the flesh, which are adultery, fornication, uncleanness, lasciviousness, idolatry, witchcraft, hatred, variance, emulations, wrath, strife, seditions, heresies, envying, murders, drunkenness, reveling, etc. These have spread throughout the world, and committing these evils means not being allowed into heaven. The evil of the flesh separated them from God, which was Satan's plan from the beginning.

The sadness is that many forgot who created us and that there is a superior spiritual force over all. God has allowed the world to continue on a destructive course, only to see his chosen people standing with their righteous faith being mutilated by evildoers. The idea of antichrists and evil leaders thinking that they had a right to implement decisions causing the deaths of so many is in violation of God's commandments. Little did the ruthless leaders realize that they would never see the Kingdom of God! God in all of his wisdom loves sinners, and because he loves us his plan is coming to pass. In her book *Will America Survive?* author E. G. White writes (Chapter 33, "Father of Lies"):

> *With the earliest history of man, Satan began his efforts to deceive our race. He who had incited rebellion in heaven desired to bring the inhabitants of*

## Chapter 7: WE BELIEVE

*earth to unite with him in his warfare against the government of God. Adam and Eve had been perfectly happy in obedience to the law of God, and this fact was a constant testimony against the claim which Satan had urged in heaven, that God's law was oppressive, and opposed to the good of His creatures. And, furthermore, Satan's envy was excited as he looked upon the beautiful home prepared for the sinless pair. He determined to cause their fall, that, having separated them from God, and brought them under his own power, he might gain possession of the earth, and here establish his kingdom, in opposition to the Most High.*

*Had Satan revealed himself in his real character, he would have been repulsed at once, for Adam and Eve had been warned against this dangerous foe; but he worked in the dark, concealing his purpose, that he might more effectually accomplish his object. Employing as his medium the serpent, then a creature of fascinating appearance, he addressed himself to Eve, "Hath God said, ye shall not eat of every tree of the garden?" Genesis 3:1. Had Eve refrained from entering into argument with the tempter, she would have been safe; but she ventured to parley with him, and fell a victim to his wiles. It is thus that many are still overcome. They doubt and argue concerning the requirements of God, and instead of obeying the divine commands, they accept human theories, which but disguise the devices of Satan.*

## SIN

It's sad to see how mankind has destroyed God's original vision of human life, loving, peaceful, and perfect. Mankind forgot about the disobedience of Adam and the true destiny for human beings. Mankind was born with free will in matters of good and evil, and evil has overcome this world. Satan has succeeded in his intentions towards human beings. The sin of Adam came at a high cost: evil spreading like a wildfire, a fire that's uncontrollable, with mankind caught in the middle and no way out. Totally consumed by it, sinful humans definitely didn't have the blessing of remaining unsinged, like Shadrach, Meshach, and Abednego (Daniel 3:25-26). With evil penetrating through the darkness, nobody even imagined what was happening. The Devil consumed the souls of those who *wished* to be evil, because in that case goodness couldn't overcome it.

God, looking upon what he had intended for his chosen people as they remained steadfast in their faith, is now finally about to bring an end to sin. Loving and compassionate, God had a plan for his chosen people to be saved and receive eternal life. He needed a human being to be the sacrificial lamb for our sins. The Precious One was the only one worthy and able to deal with sin. The Precious One is coming back to deal with evil for the last time. At the beginning it was all about good and evil, and of course we know that evil prevailed. The Precious One will fight the last battle between good and evil, with the victory to our Lord and personal Savior.

The Precious One was anointed as a sinless redeemer for mankind. He was resurrected from his human soul to a spiritual

## Chapter 7: WE BELIEVE

soul and now reigns with God. Blessed with the Holy Spirit, the Precious One knew what his mission was. He wanted humans to understand the path we must take to have eternal life, because sin cannot enter the holy Kingdom of God. The Precious One was the first human being to enter the Kingdom of God as a spiritual soul. The mystery was solved when the Precious One paved the way and showed all other believers how to be saved. The Precious One said it all in John 14:1-4, 6:

> *Let not your heart be troubled: ye believe in God, believe also in me. In my Father's house are many mansions: if it were not so, I would have told you. I go to prepare a place for you. And if I go and prepare a place for you, I will come again, and receive you unto myself; that where I am, there ye may be also. And whither I go ye know, and the way ye know. ... I am the way, the truth, and the life: no man cometh unto the Father, but by me.*

The Precious One is coming back for the true believers, not the 50% believers. A friend told me that when the Precious One returns, we had better be a 100% believer because less than 100% will not pass. We had better pass the prerequisite courses that the Precious One left for us to complete at 100%, showing a strong A, meaning accepted and not rejected. Time is running out and the Devil knows it—that's why he is gathering as many souls as possible to enter Devil's Heaven. We all may have *visited* Devil's Heaven, but the test is whether we make it out in time!

God's plan was in place for his chosen people to have a chance of everlasting life through the Precious One, the lamb sacrificed for sin. As for 50% believers, your path is already chosen!

Author E. G. White continues in her book, *Will America Survive?* in Chapter 33, "Father of Lies":

> *God has given in His word decisive evidence that He will punish the transgressors of His law. Those who flatter themselves that He is too merciful to execute justice upon the sinner have only to look to the cross of Calvary. The death of the spotless Son of God testifies that "the wages of sin is death," that every violation of God's law must receive its just retribution. Christ the sinless became sin for man. He bore the guilt of transgression, and the hiding of His Father's face, until His heart was broken and his life crushed out. All this sacrifice was made that sinners might be redeemed. In no other way could man be freed from the penalty of sin. And every soul that refuses to become partaker of the atonement provided at such a cost must bear, in his own person, the guilt and punishment of transgression.*

Judgment Day is about the second death. When all will be judged for their faith and works, the wicked and evil ones' names will not be found in the book of life and they will be cast into the lake of fire. E. G. White goes on in her book, *Will America Survive?* in Chapter 33, "Father of Lies":

> *In consequence of Adam's sin, death passed upon the whole human race. All alike go down into the grave.*

## Chapter 7: WE BELIEVE

*And through the provisions of the plan of salvation, all are to be brought forth from their graves. "There shall be a resurrection of the dead, both of the just and unjust" (Acts 24:15); "for as in Adam all die, even so in Christ shall all be made alive." 1 Corinthians 15:22. But a distinction is made between the two classes that are brought forth. "All that are in the graves shall hear His voice, and shall come forth; they that have done good, unto the resurrection of life; and they that have done evil, unto the resurrection of damnation." John 5:28-29. They who have been "accounted worthy" of the resurrection of life are "blessed and holy." "On such the second death hath no power." Revelation 20:6. But those who have not, through repentance and faith, secured pardon, must receive the penalty of transgression—"the wages of sin." They suffer punishment varying in duration and intensity, "according to their works," but finally ending in the second death. Since it is impossible for God, consistently with His justice and mercy, to save the sinner in his sins, He deprives him of the existence which his transgressions have forfeited, and of which he has proved himself unworthy. Says an inspired writer, "Yet a little while, and the wicked shall not be; yea, thou shalt diligently consider his place, and it shall not be." And another declares, "They shall be as though they had not been." Psalms 37:10; Obadiah 16. Covered with infamy, they sink into hopeless, eternal oblivion.*

*Thus will be made an end of sin, with all the woe and ruin which have resulted from it.*

Sin has become the standard, but I hope that the 50% believers jump the fence to become true believers. God hates the sin but loves the sinner! Your hole is growing so deep with no way out. *"No man can serve two masters: for either he will hate the one, and love the other; or else he will hold to the one, and despise the other. Ye cannot serve God and mammon"* (Matthew 6:24). Many people in this world have sat back and become complacent instead of taking a proactive stance. We cannot forget the wrath of God in the Old Testament. We are living in difficult and trying times, in which Satan has been going nonstop in all situations. We are living under a Satanic system worse than Sodom and Gomorrah.

If we could gaze down on Earth through a window from heaven, what positive picture could we paint? God is sending us another truth to save His children. The Mark of the Beast will force us to make a choice. If we are walking in obedience to God and seeking first his Kingdom and his righteousness, all the other things will be added unto us (Matthew 6:33). But for sinners who think they are saved, God says, *"But as for them whose heart walketh after the heart of their detestable things and their abominations, I will recompense their way upon their own heads, saith the Lord God"* (Ezekiel 11:21).

Human beings will know their destiny when the Precious One returns, and if we didn't pass the prerequisite courses it means we probably have taken the Antichrist's mark. God knows our destiny already. Is our hole filling up with God's love or is it so deep in Devil's Heaven that we don't care to fix it? The Seal of God or the Mark of the Beast, which do we prefer? The Precious One paid the price for sin so that we could be saved and have a chance for everlasting life.

Chapter 7: WE BELIEVE

## SECOND COMFORTER

The Precious One left us with prerequisite courses that have to be passed during the End Times. It is critical that those who are living that want everlasting life must receive the second Comforter. The Precious One knows by our light whether God has sent us the second Comforter. The second Comforter reveals whether we love one another and whether evil has no place in our hearts. We must pass the prerequisite courses or be forgotten, our names erased from the Book of Life. That will be an important final exam during the End Times.

The Precious One was the only person with the right to pray to the Father to send us the second Comforter and he has given us plenty of time to receive it. Without the second Comforter we will not be resurrected to God's family. The Precious One was the first to be resurrected to God's family. He was a human being and now is a spiritual being. All believers should strive to be like him, so their bodies can become spiritual and reside with God, the Precious One, and other blessed souls.

Nobody will see God if they are still in Devil's Heaven. If we are living during the End Times we will witness the final close to man's government. It is time for God's Kingdom and government to rule! Satan knows he has only a short time to destroy God's people and he is working overtime to get as many souls into Devil's Heaven as he can. God is giving all sinners a final chance to receive eternal life at the end of man's control. We need to repent of our sins and get out of Devil's Heaven!

## REALITY

I wrote this book for all believers, whether 50% or 100%. This is our wake-up call. It isn't about religion, nationality, race, or language, I truly believe that all religions have fallen short of the true Church of God. It's really about what's in our hearts. Do we love God? Do we try to be like the Precious One, loving one another? This wake-up call is different and final because it concerns eternal life. We can't keep extending it ten more minutes. It is the final wake-up call!

When we stop and see what is truly happening in the world, this wake-up call will become important to our future. WWIII will happen and two billion people will be killed. The Antichrist is real and he will deceive nearly everyone. Understand that during the End Times, whether we are killed or not, as long as we are beheaded for the witness of the Precious One and the Word of God and have not worshipped the beast, we will live and reign with the Precious One for a thousand years.

When we think of all the many loved ones we've lost who believed in the Precious One as their Lord and personal Savior, don't we want to be part of that exclusive club that receives eternal life? Wake up, my brothers and sisters in Christ! 100% believers have some common threads that unite them: they believe in God and his Son, the Precious One; they have repented of their sins and have been born again. We aren't even the same person when we're born again. We see things much clearer and we know by our testimonies that the Precious One is alive and abides in us.

I have always felt that something had to be written about the Precious One's return to earth. I believe most people lack the knowledge of what is to come. If people don't open their eyes the Mark of the Beast will be very easy to take. We are all trying to survive in this world, but the responsibility to continue to spread the Good News about God falls on the shoulders of the 100% believers. It is easy to tell who is a 100% or 50% believer. The 50% believers look into the mirror to disguise their sin with makeup. It doesn't matter if they place light or heavy makeup on their face, for a sin is a sin and has no degrees or levels. It's a mask that one wears to try to conceal their sin. Behind the mask, covered with makeup, is darkness. The 100% believers look into the mirror and they don't need any makeup. They need no mask to hide behind. Their natural beauty illuminates, like a light shining brightly!

The 50% believers should start using makeup remover to clean their face (repent of their sins). Then the natural beauty will shine as they enter into the light. In 2 Corinthians 5:17 we read, *"Therefore if any man be in Christ, he is a new creature: old things are passed away; behold, all things are become new."* 50% believers, it's time to be reborn and make everything right in our lives. If we are 50% believers during the End Times, we never made it out of darkness to the light, we failed the final exam. If we don't open our hearts to learn what will happen and why, then the Devil will win. Let's be sure we are God's chosen children and that we believe.

**We Believe:**

1. There is only one God, whom we love, honor, and obey.
2. There is only one redeemer for our sins, the Precious One.
3. We need to go through the Son, the Precious One, to get to the Father and be free from sin.
4. We must repent, be baptized, and pray, as the Devil will try to destroy us.
5. We need to love one another and receive the Precious One's Comforter rewarded by God.
6. We must continue to minister to others, have faith, do good works, and spread the Good News.
7. We are God's chosen people, 100%, and hope to be blessed with eternal life.

## We Believe

**John 16:31**
*"Jesus answered them, 'Do ye now believe?'"*

Brothers and Sisters in Christ
United through the end
One common thread ties us
We Believe, We Believe

Wars all around
Nations dying left and right
The false prophet finally showing
Satan's running with power and might

## Chapter 7: WE BELIEVE

Wanted to be kings of kings, lords of lords
But still devilish and deceiving
Marked his people for all to see
Searching for you and me

Satan's army can't compete
Army of God's impossible to beat
Dying for our beliefs
Eternal life we will receive

Brothers and Sisters in Christ
United through the end
One common thread ties us
We Believe, We Believe

Satan's looking to devour all
Anyone who stands in his way
Killed God's two End Time Witnesses
What a mistake he made

Didn't realize who's in charge
The Precious One is Truth, Water & Blood
Will destroy Satan and his army
We're blessed God's seal is upon us all

Brothers and Sisters in Christ
United through the end
One common thread ties us
We Believe, We Believe

Shut down Satan and his fleet
Poor followers now you see
Lost your soul to the wicked one
Can't undo what is done

> We waited for this time to come
> Faith has brought us through
> Lost loved ones but we know
> Work and faith, together soon
>
> Brothers and Sisters in Christ
> United through the end
> One common thread ties us
> We Believe, We Believe

I truly believe that all God's children have many testimonies to tell. We must spread the Good News about the Precious One. I know that we will go through many trials and tribulations. I have been through many trials and tribulations moving to Atlanta, Georgia. I have been through so many operations that I can't remember the exact dates or years. My goddaughter was correct when she told me, "You have been sick ever since moving to Atlanta." She was correct, the Devil has been trying to destroy my spirit, but I serve a good God who has always had my back. The Devil couldn't win and break my relationship with the Precious One. I realized the Devil had been working double time to break my spirit, trying to stop this book from being completed. My trials and tribulations have only made me stronger in faith, so that I sit back with a smile on my face for the Devil to see! With everything that I have been through, I thank God for lifting me up and always being that partner that I needed. I thank God for giving us the Precious One so that I may strive for eternal life. When you have the two blessed advocates abiding in you (Holy Spirit and the second Comforter), you have achieved the winning combination and scored a touchdown to eternal life!

## Chapter 7: WE BELIEVE

Remember what 1 John 2:22-29 says:

*Who is a liar but he that denieth that Jesus is the Christ? He is antichrist, that denieth the Father and the Son. Whosoever denieth the Son, the same hath not the Father: (but) he that acknowledgeth the Son hath the Father also. Let that therefore abide in you, which ye have heard from the beginning. If that which ye have heard from the beginning shall remain in you, ye also shall continue in the Son, and in the Father. And this is the promise that he hath promised us, even eternal life. These things have I written unto you concerning them that seduce you. But the anointing which ye have received of him abideth in you, and ye need not that any man teach you: but as the same anointing teacheth you of all things, and is truth, and is no lie, and even as it hath taught you, ye shall abide in him. And now, little children, abide in him; that, when he shall appear, we may have confidence, and not be ashamed before him at his coming. If ye know that he is righteous, ye know that every one that doeth righteousness is born of him.*

When the Antichrist appears, God's children will know. We can't take the Mark of the Beast. Buying or selling with the Mark is something we can't do. We must flee, young and old, for victory is ours. Open your eyes and observe it all—the world isn't getting better! United powers are making it easier for a One World leader to emerge, but don't be deceived. This is God's plan, a plan revealed long ago. Good and evil had to fight it out, and the

Precious One will set it right. Fighting the Antichrist is a battle only for the Precious One. Good and evil must battle, because God never intended his people to live like this. The Precious One will finish this battle at Armageddon. God is the Alpha and the Omega and it's time to finish his story. Evil will be gone once and for all, that is God's plan—a world that is sin-free and enjoys the life that God always wanted for his chosen people.

I pray that this book will enlighten all to an open discussion about the End Times. It was written to open our eyes to the situations in the world. There may come a time when we must get back to the basics of survival. As believers we know that the Precious One is returning and that we cannot take the Mark of the Beast because we have the seal of God upon us. The world will not get any better, as indicated by the sounding of the Sixth Trumpet. We must begin to prepare for what will be dealt to us. If we are living during the End Times and the Antichrist is in control, we know what to expect and what we must do. I pray that everyone will make the right choice. This book was orchestrated by the power of the Holy Spirit. I am just a servant being obedient to the Word. If you have finished this book and truly understand the message, then I have succeeded, even if we disagree on some issues. We are living in the generation that will see the Antichrist. We all need to know what is coming. WWIII will be huge and explosive. Two billion will die! Please don't take this for granted. The Sixth Trumpet has sounded and a major war, WWIII, will be the last war before our Savior returns.

## Chapter 7: WE BELIEVE

Always remember John 3:16-21:

*For God so loved the world, that he gave his only begotten Son, that whosoever believeth in him should not perish, but have everlasting life. For God sent not his Son into the world to condemn the world; but that the world through him might be saved. He that believeth on him is not condemned: but he that believeth not is condemned already, because he hath not believed in the name of the only begotten Son of God. And this is the condemnation, that light is come into the world, and men loved darkness rather than light, because their deeds were evil. For every one that doeth evil hateth the light, neither cometh to the light, lest his deeds should be reproved. But he that doeth truth cometh to the light, that his deeds may be made manifest, that they are wrought in God.*

### Eternal Life

Eternal Life
Striven for
Eternal Life
Forever more

Devil's Heaven
Quick to pull us in
Devil taking too many souls
Repent and get out of the hole

## WE BELIEVE® The Precious One Is Coming Back

<u>Bloodlines</u> of Jesus
We must have
Jesus will not pick us
If tainted blood is bad

<u>Judgment Day</u> awakes
Hallelujah, Amen
All the evil ones
Can't walk through the pearly gates

Sixth <u>Sounding Trumpet</u>
As Antichrist arise
All bowing with praise
Deceiving devil in disguise

<u>Mark of the Beast</u>
Blinded to their defeat
The Precious One can't undo
The Mark that's on you

<u>End Time Witnesses</u>
Preached the word
Trying to reach 50% believers
Saving their souls from hell

<u>We Believe</u> through the end
Now we know the truth
The Winning Path, Eternal Life
Which path is best for you

Look for
future books in the

*We Believe*

series.